Unscheduled Departure

T.M. Franklin

Unscheduled Departure

Copyright © T.M. Franklin, 2015
All Rights Reserved

The right of T.M. Franklin to be identified as the author of this work has been asserted by her under the Copyright Amendment (Moral Rights) Act 2000.

This work is copyrighted. All rights are reserved. Apart from any use as permitted under the Copyright Act of 1968, no part may be reproduced, copied, scanned, stored in a retrieval system, recorded or transmitted, in any form or by any means, without the prior written permission of the author.

All characters and events in this Book – even those sharing the same name as (or based upon) real people – are entirely fictional. Any resemblance to real persons, living or dead is purely coincidental. No person, brand or corporation mentioned in this Book should be taken to have endorsed this Book nor should the events surrounding them be considered in any way factual.

This Book is a work of fiction and should be read as such.

Cover images licensed by
©DollarPhotoClub.com/chungking
©DollarPhotoClub.com/spongeman
©Depositphotos.com/agsandrew

Cover design by T.M. Franklin

Originally part of the *Frequent Flyers* collection, published by Bolero Books.

Visit the Author's web site at
www.TMFranklin.com

UNSCHEDULED DEPARTURE

T.M. FRANKLIN

"Fantastic writing and storytelling, pleasantly reminiscent of The Twilight Zone." – Olivia, Goodreads Reviewer

Rowan Elliott is devastated when her boyfriend, Finn, tells her he's moving across the country to take over the family business, and thrilled when he changes his mind at the last minute and gets off the plane.

But then things get . . . weird. Finn's acting strange, and Ro's getting mysterious phone calls that have her questioning if her boyfriend's really who she thinks he is. As Ro races to figure out what's going on, she discovers it's more complicated than she could have ever imagined.

And if she's not careful, she could lose her Finn forever.

Also by T.M. Franklin

The MORE Trilogy
MORE
The Guardians
TWELVE

The New Super Humans
Super Humans
Super Powers
Super Natural
Super Heroes

Standalone Novels
Cutlass
How to Get Ainsley Bishop to Fall in Love With You
Second Chances: A Holiday Romance

Short Stories
A Piece of Cake
Coming Soon - Drive Me Crazy

Find out more at www.TMFranklin.com

Unscheduled Departure

5:12 AM
Tuesday

Finn whipped the door open before I could even knock, eyes frantic and dark hair tousled like he'd been tugging at it again.

"What's wrong?" I asked.

"You're late."

I frowned. "Only five minutes. I texted y—"

"Sorry... sorry, I know." Finn ran both hands through his already crazy hair, yanking it into wild spikes around his head. "I mean *I'm* late. I'm going to be late. I can't find my stupid wallet." He whirled through the living room, tossing pillows that looked like they'd been tossed several times already. The living room was a mess of stacked-up boxes and furniture gathered from the other rooms. There'd been a mix-up with the movers, so I'd be meeting them the next day to make sure everything got picked up. Finn couldn't change his flight, and I'd assured him there was no need.

He fumbled through an open box, dropping towels on the floor. "I set it aside. I know I did," he said. "I put it somewhere—"

"Where you wouldn't forget it." I smiled when he looked up at me with frantic eyes. "It's okay. Take a breath. We'll find it."

Finn obediently inhaled, straightening and closing his eyes for a moment. "What am I doing?" he asked quietly.

"We'll find the—"

"No." He rubbed his hands over his face and let out a long, shaky breath. "I mean, what am I doing? I'm moving to the other side of the country, Ro."

I reached out to touch his hand and he gripped it tightly.

"It's what you wanted," I said, my heart pounding heavily. "Your family needs you." I said the words, even though we both knew I didn't really believe them.

He smiled sadly. "But you—"

I slid my hand up his cheek and smoothed the hair over his ear. "I'll be here. Right here. I'm not going anywhere." I forced myself to meet his stormy, grey eyes and fought back my own misgivings about Finn leaving. "We'll be fine. We can do this." I smiled without feeling it.

2,743 miles.

Well, 2,743 miles from Seattle to Washington DC. Another thirty-five or so across the border to his family home in Virginia where he'd be living. Since his father's death, Finn's brother Aiden had run the family business, a real-estate development firm based in Springfield. But Aiden had disappeared with the office manager— a married woman nearly twice his age— and had called only to say he was sorry, he just couldn't take it anymore, and he and Meg were going to spend some time in South America to find some purpose in their lives.

Which meant . . .

Well, I *thought* it meant that it was time to sell the business, pocket the cash and move on. Finn's mother had other ideas, however. She'd called in tears, begging him to come take over —just temporarily, until they could figure out what to do next. I knew there was nothing temporary about it, though. Finn's mom had always wanted him back home, and had never approved of him moving to Seattle to study software engineering at the University of Washington.

Finn was good at the business end of things. He was raised in board meetings and learned at an early age the art of the deal. But he didn't enjoy it. He preferred working with technology, solving problems and writing code, instead of sitting in endless business meetings.

But he also loved his mother and was devoted to his family. And since his sister was still in high school, he didn't see an alternative to giving in to his mother's pleas. He just couldn't say no. It wasn't an easy decision for him, and I refused to make it harder. I was a lot of things, but I tried— really tried— not to be selfish in that regard.

Which meant my boyfriend would soon be 2,743 miles away from me. And I refused to be a needy baby about it.

"It'll be okay," I said, my voice, at least, firm and sure,

Unscheduled Departure

even if the rest of me wasn't. "We'll Skype and text. And I'll try to fly out for Spring Break."

"And I'll try and be back for Christmas," he said, although I doubted that would happen. Once he got involved in Beckett Enterprises, there would be no getting out. They'd need him, and he wouldn't be able to say no. It wasn't in Finn's nature.

"It'll be fine," I said, willing myself to believe it.

I lifted up on my tiptoes and wrapped my arms around his neck, and he met me halfway in a soft kiss. I indulged in a moment of sorrow, a softening against Finn as his strong arms held me up, a sinking into the kiss and the feeling of Finn surrounding me, filling me. Suddenly desperate, I gripped his hair, pulling him closer as the kiss deepened, grew hungry and pained— as if we both knew it would be our last.

Last for a while. I refused to believe anything else.

We broke apart, breath harsh against each other's lips. "We've got to go," Finn said, his voice low and graveled. He cursed, dipping his head until our foreheads touched. "I still have to find my wallet."

"We'll find it," I said as I pulled away to rifle through a stack of papers on the end table.

5:27 AM

"Why in the world would you put your wallet in the freezer, Finnegan?"

"Not my name. And we don't have time for ridiculous questions." He snatched the item in question out of my hand and jammed it into his back pocket. His lips twitched as he fought a smile, then he lurched forward to kiss me soundly. "Let's go."

He reached for his coffee cup, hitching his carry on onto his shoulder at the same time. Which proved to be a mistake, as he fumbled the cup, a trail of milky coffee splashing down the sleeve of his white shirt.

I covered my mouth to hide the laugh.

He saw it anyway. He grabbed a wad of paper towels off

the kitchen counter and blotted the stain.

"You need to change?" I asked.

"No time. It's fine," he replied, giving the towels one last squeeze before tossing them in the kitchen garbage can. "Two points," he said with a grin, before he grabbed my hand to drag me out the front door.

5:29 AM

"Did you lock the door?"
"I thought you locked it."
"Damn it!"

6:03 AM

We dashed down the airport corridor, narrowly dodging a man pulling a suitcase. Finn glanced back, his sweaty hand slipping on mine as he dragged me around a corner.

I barely kept from tripping over my own feet. "Ticket?"

"Got it!" he shouted.

"Liquids?"

"Ready!" He fumbled with his free hand in the front pocket of his carryon to pull out the plastic bag.

"Line!"

"Wha—?" He looked back at me as if in slow motion, though his feet kept moving.

"Line!" I yanked my hand from his to point beyond him and he whirled, barely managing to avoid barreling into the back of the security line.

We stopped, breathing heavily.

"Thanks," he said between pants.

"No problem."

Usually, when you're in a hurry to go somewhere, you just . . . go there. Of course, the airport is the exception to that rule. We stood fidgeting as the line crawled forward, Finn checking his watch every two seconds.

"I'm not going to make it," he muttered.

"You'll make it." I straightened his collar, which didn't need straightening, simply to keep my hands moving— as if

Unscheduled Departure

that could distract me. "You got everything?"

"Yeah. Yeah, I think so." He reached for my hand and pressed it against his lips. "You okay?"

I nodded, swallowing down tears. The security line moved forward at a snail's pace– too fast.

"Call when you land, okay?" I asked. "Doesn't matter what time it is."

"I will." He kissed me. "Don't forget to call your mom tomorrow."

"Crap. Yeah, thanks." I added the reminder to my phone.

Another step forward...and another. Only a family of four and a little old man stood between us and the scanners. The mom at the front of the line was arguing with her son, who didn't want to take off his shoes.

Mom won. Well, the kid took off his shoes anyway. He also screamed bloody murder, so maybe it was a wash.

"I should go," I whispered, blinking rapidly.

Finn pulled me tight against him as he toed off his own shoes. "I'm sorry we don't have more time."

There would never be enough time.

"It's better this way. Quick, like a band-aid, right?" I clung to him for a moment, breathing him in.

"Next!" The security officer obviously didn't have romantic bone in his body.

"I've got to go." Finn kissed me one more time, traced a finger down my cheek, and then he was through the X-ray machine...down the hall... one more look and around the corner. Gone.

"Miss, you'll have to step out of line if you're not a ticketed passenger." The unromantic TSA agent arched a brow at me.

I nodded and ducked under the barrier, glancing back one last time, but there was no sign of Finn. I was being ridiculous. I knew that. He was getting on a plane and our lives would be different— harder, maybe— but everything would be fine.

I hoped.

My phone buzzed and I smiled when I saw a text from Finn.

I miss you already.

I wove through the crowd to an empty spot along the wall. I leaned against a support post and toed absently at a black scuff mark on the tile floor as I texted him back.

I miss you too.

I hesitated, then added *Please don't go.*

What was I doing? My thumb hovered over the *Send* button, and I was filled with a sudden rush of yearning, an irrational fear that if he left, Finn would never come back. I wavered, unsure what to do as my thumb twitched over the screen.

Delete.

Send.

The image flickered before my eyes, words blurring through my tears. My heart pounded, tongue sticking to the roof of my mouth as I swayed a little on my feet. I could hear blood pounding in my ears, louder and faster, as I stared down at the phone screen.

Delete.

Send.

Finally, with a sheepish sigh and a shake of my head, I wiped the tears from my eyes, deleted the second sentence and pushed *Send*.

We'd be fine.

6:45 AM

I wasn't sure why I waited around until take-off. It wasn't like I could actually see the plane from where I was, let alone spot Finn looking sad and forlorn, waving bleakly through the window. Okay, maybe that was a little bit of wishful thinking, misery loves company and all that, but down deep in places I didn't like other people to see, I had to admit I hoped he was suffering, too. Just a little bit.

That probably made me a horrible person, but in my defense, I only indulged in my self-pity party for a few miserable minutes.

I stared unseeingly out the big windows overlooking the tarmac and the brown grass of the field beyond, and let out a

Unscheduled Departure

heavy sigh before I checked the time.

6:46. The plane was in the air.

Finn was gone.

I sighed again and fought the tears I could feel pricking at my eyes. I wasn't going to cry. Finn was gone, but we could make it through.

Finn was gone.

I turned around, repeating the words like a mantra in my head.

Finn was . . .

He was . . .

Finn was standing right in front of me.

I froze, and I swore my heart stopped, my mouth hanging open as I stared at him. "What . . .? How . . .?" I reached out toward him, then snatched my hand back, half-afraid I was imagining him.

Finn's lips twitched and he dropped his bag, crossing to me in two big steps. He swept me into his arms, and I let out a soft gasp at the familiar scent of his shampoo, tucking my face into his neck as he held me tight. He pulled away only to move right back in and kiss me, stealing my breath again at the warmth of his lips, his touch.

After a long moment, he broke the kiss and took a deep breath. "I didn't go," he whispered against my skin.

I laughed, a little tingly and giddy. Lightheaded. "Yeah, I got that." I reached up to tangle my fingers in his hair, searching his face for answers. "But why not?"

He looked into my eyes, searching and quiet for a moment. "I couldn't go. I got your text and I just . . ." He looked away and wiped a hand over his face. "I'll have to talk to my mom, tell her I'm not coming. We'll just have to figure something else out."

My mind swam with guilt and relief. "Are you sure? I don't want to cause problems—"

"This is my choice," he said firmly, pulling me a little closer and pressing his forehead to mine. "You are my choice. *We* are. The rest . . . we'll figure it out. It'll be okay."

I let my eyes flutter closed and leaned into him, my fingers drifting up and down his back under his jacket. He made a little humming sound and kissed my neck.

"What now?" I asked.

Finn let out a little laugh and stepped back, taking my hand and interlacing our fingers. "Now, we go try to figure out how to get my luggage back. Then, I drop you at school and call to cancel the movers." He frowned. "Then I call my mom."

I winced in sympathy. "Good luck with that one."

7:45 AM

Turns out, it's not as complicated as you'd think retrieving luggage from an airplane headed across the country. It wasn't free, but the airline agreed to put Finn's bags on the next plane headed back from Chicago.

He'd put off calling his mom, figuring he had until his plane landed in Washington—still several hours away—before he really had to do it. I didn't push it. I didn't envy Finn that conversation. We'd brainstormed alternatives as we drove back from the airport, stalled in rush hour traffic. My first class was at eight, and Finn dodged between slow-moving cars to try and better our time, ignoring the honks and one-finger salutes.

"How about your uncle?" I asked. "Your mom's brother— what's his name?"

"Uncle Gary?" Finn shook his head as he swerved into the carpool lane. "They haven't spoken in years. Not since dad died. He wanted to take over then, but Mom doesn't really trust him."

"Well, if she's so adamant you keep the company, why doesn't *she* run it?"

Finn laughed humorlessly. "Good question." He glanced at me sideways. "Mom's too busy with charity work."

"Charity work?"

He shrugged. "Well, that and hair appointments. Nail appointments. Meetings with her spiritual consultant. Facialist. Pet psychic."

"Your mom has a pet psychic." I gave him a bland look.

Finn's lips quirked. "Well, technically, it's for Mr.

Unscheduled Departure

Nibbles."

"I can't believe a chihuahua needs a psychic."

"You obviously haven't met Mr. Nibbles." Finn caught my eye and we both burst out laughing. "He has a lot of unresolved issues from past lives, apparently."

I shook my head sympathetically. "Oh, the bones that were never chewed. The stuffed animals that went unhumped."

"He's sure making up for that now. My old G.I. Joe won't be wearing white at his wedding."

I couldn't keep down the giggles. "Poor Mr. Nibbles. He only wants to be loved."

Finn shuddered. "Okay, we need to stop talking about my mother's dog now. I'm pretty sure this might scar me for life." He cut across four lanes to get to the exit and I gripped the seat, bracing myself against the door.

"Remind me to drive next time, Phineas," I muttered.

"Not my name," he said, jerking to a stop as the light changed. "And we'd still be sitting in traffic if you were driving."

I rolled my eyes instead of responding, too happy that Finn was sitting next to me to even argue the point. I looked out the window at the passing businesses as we navigated the U-District, thinking about all that had happened that morning. Over the past few days, I'd spent a lot of time wondering if Finn and I would make it, if we'd survive a long-distance relationship at all. In just a couple of hours everything had changed. We had a future. And all because . . .

"Finn?"

"Yeah?"

I reached across the seat to take his hand. "Don't get me wrong. I'm so glad you're here. You don't even know."

He smiled and winked at me. "Yeah. Me too."

"But what changed your mind?" I asked.

He signaled and turned a corner before he answered. "I was feeling off all morning. But in the end, I guess it was your text."

I rubbed a thumb over the back of his hand. "When I said I'd miss you?" That was so sweet.

"When you asked me not to go," he replied.

What?

"Wait a second. I didn't. I didn't ask you." *What was he talking about?*

Finn glanced at me, brow furrowed. "You did. You said you were going to miss me, then you said, 'don't go.' When I saw that—"

"But I didn't," I let go of his hand and pulled my phone out of my purse. "I mean, I was going to. I wanted to. But I didn't." I thumbed my phone open, flipped to my text messages. "I couldn't ask that of you. I couldn't be the one—" I scrolled through my texts, stabbing my finger at the thread with Finn. "I couldn't . . ."

I miss you already.

I miss you too.

"I couldn't . . ."

Please don't go.

"Ro?" I jolted, and realized he must have called my name more than once.

"You okay?" he asked.

I cleared my throat and looked back down at my phone.

Please don't go.

But I didn't . . . I hadn't.

"I don't understand," I said quietly. "I mean, I thought I deleted that."

This time Finn reached across the seat to take my hand. He pressed it to his lips, smiling against my skin. "I'm glad you didn't," he said.

I smiled weakly. "Yeah. Yeah, me too."

I thought for sure I'd deleted the text. I'd agonized over it, but in the end, I decided I couldn't put that kind of pressure on Finn. I felt bad that, in the end, I had. At the same time, Finn was now sitting next to me, so a small part of me felt victorious. Ecstatic.

Selfish.

I hadn't meant to, but I'd kept Finn in Seattle.

"I wanted to stay," he said, as if he'd read my mind. "I wanted to, Ro. It was my choice."

I nodded and turned to look out the window. The decision

was made, and feeling guilty served no purpose anyway. I stared down at my phone, the text glowing. . . accusing, until the screen went black.

7:57 AM

Finn ignored the No Parking sign and pulled right up to the front of Guthrie Hall, home of the Department of Psychology. I leaned across the console to kiss him quickly goodbye.

"See you later," he said.

I smirked. "Later, Finnester."

He got kind of a funny look on his face, then said, "Not my name." He bopped me on the nose before I ducked out of the car to run up the steps, hoping I wouldn't be late for the pop quiz that everyone knew was coming.

Finn took off to grab some coffee and make some much-needed phone calls before he had to be back to pick me up in an hour. I paused, frowning as I watched the car turn the corner.

He'd kissed me . . . weirdly.

I didn't know how else to describe it. Maybe he was distracted. Maybe it was because I was in a hurry. His lips looked the same, felt the same, but something was different. Weird.

Ugh. I obviously needed more coffee.

I shook off the strange feeling and raced down the hall, taking my seat in the lecture hall mere seconds before the clock hit the top of the hour and Professor Simons announced the pop quiz.

9:07 AM

"How'd it go?" Finn asked as I got into the car after class.

I shrugged. "Fine. I guess. Pop quizzes aren't worth much, so I'm not that worried."

Finn nodded as he pulled away from the curb. He headed to the diner around the corner from my ten o'clock English class and I thumbed through my phone, not looking for anything in particular. We parked and made our way into the restaurant, ordering coffee and breakfast sandwiches at the counter since I was relatively short on time.

"Did you talk to your mom?" I asked.

Finn took a sip of his coffee— black and disgusting— as I added more sugar to my own cup.

"Yeah," he replied. "She . . . wasn't happy."

"What's she going to do?"

"I'm not sure. I suggested she take over or turn it over to the board. Maybe sell out— there's another developer who's been chomping at the bit to buy us out since dad died."

"Is she willing to do that?"

Finn sighed and tore a piece of bread from the corner of his sandwich, crumbling it between his fingers. "Not yet. She may not have a choice, if she doesn't want to take the reins herself." He shrugged out of his coat and draped it over the back of his chair. I picked up my sandwich and Finn reached down to unbutton his sleeve and roll up the cuff.

Wait a second.

I set my sandwich back down. "Did you go home?"

He rolled up his other sleeve. "No. I just got some coffee and waited for you."

"But—" I reached out and grabbed his wrist, unrolling his sleeve. His pale, yellow sleeve, unstained by coffee. "When did you change your shirt?"

"What?"

"Your shirt. You spilled coffee on it this morning."

He nodded slowly. "Yeah? I know. I was there."

I sat back, confused. "But I thought—" I reached for his other arm. Maybe I had the wrong sleeve. "I thought it was white."

"Ro, what's the big deal?" Finn asked, pulling away to roll his sleeves back up again. "Yes, I spilled coffee on my sleeve this morning. Which is why I changed my shirt before we left for the airport."

"What?" I blinked. That wasn't what happened. Was it? "No. You wiped it off. We were in a hurry."

"I changed, Ro."

"But it was white. Your shirt was white."

"Right. And now it's yellow. Because I changed it." Finn's forehead creased with confusion. I didn't blame him. I was pretty confused myself.

"God, what's wrong with me? Sorry." I muttered, wiping a hand over my face. "I'm just tired, I guess. I could have sworn—" I laughed, shaking my hand. "Nothing. It's nothing."

First the text I thought I'd deleted. Now the mystery of the missing coffee stain.

"It's not a big deal," Finn said with a laugh. "It's just a shirt."

"Right. Yeah."

He lifted my hand to his lips and kissed the tip of my index finger. It was something he always did and it never failed to make me smile, although it made my best friend Lindsay roll her eyes and make gagging noises. I pushed my finger lightly against Finn's lips and he grinned.

"Love you," he said.

"Love you, too." I glanced at my phone. "But I better move it if I'm going to get to class on time."

We both picked up our sandwiches and started to eat. But my eyes still kept drifting to that unstained shirt cuff. And I couldn't calm the nervous flutter in my stomach that said something, somehow, wasn't quite right.

9:55 AM

I left Finn at the diner and headed to class, still feeling itchy— uneasy— with that heaviness in my stomach like when you're a kid and you know you're about to get in trouble.

I couldn't explain it. Couldn't understand what was wrong, really. But something deep inside me felt off. Was I forgetting things or imagining them?

I had no reason not to believe Finn about the shirt. I mean, why in the world would he lie about something like that, anyway? And the text spoke for itself. I saw it on my own phone— so obviously, I hadn't deleted it like I thought I had.

Neither thing was a big deal. But no matter how I tried to convince myself of that, I couldn't shake that odd, apprehensive feeling.

I texted Lindsay, even though I knew she had class for the next couple of hours, and asked if she wanted to get together for dinner. We hadn't seen each other for about a week, which was unheard of for us. But with Finn leaving, I'd been spending most of my time with him. Lindsay understood, but I found myself wanting to talk to her. I needed her to reassure me that I wasn't losing it or something.

My phone rang as I went to drop it back into my bag, and I frowned at the screen where it indicated a private number. I figured it was probably a telemarketer, but curiosity won out and I answered as I rounded the corner and the English building came into sight.

"Hello?"

"Ro?"

"Finn?" He sounded strange, the connection weak and crackly. "I can hardly hear you. Are you in the car?"

He said something I couldn't make out. There was a lot of noise in the background— something like a loudspeaker? But that didn't make any sense. Maybe it was the radio.

"Finn?"

The line went dead.

I stared at my phone for a moment before pulling up Finn's number and thumbing out a quick text.

Everything okay?

It took a moment for a reply.

Yeah. Then a few seconds later: *Aren't you supposed to be in class?*

I swore under my breath when I noticed the time and shoved my phone into my pocket as I started to run. I'd call Finn later, or he'd call me. I figured it couldn't have been anything too important or he would have called back. I silenced my ringer as I entered the building and tried to put the morning's weirdness out of my mind.

Unscheduled Departure

12:12 PM

I stood on the curb after my last class of the day and searched approaching traffic for Finn's car. It had been a long day, even though it was technically only half over, and I couldn't wait to get back to my apartment, crawl into my bed, and sleep for about two or three hours. Maybe days.

I was exhausted.

With Finn nowhere in sight, I realized I'd left my ringer off and pulled out my phone to find a couple of missed texts from him.

At 11:30— *Stuck in traffic on the bridge.* Then just a few minutes before noon— *Be there as soon as I can. Meet me at Perk?*

I set off for the coffee shop a block away, texting back a quick yes, then I noticed I'd also missed a call.

Private Number.

I dialed into my voicemail only to hear Finn's voice. A little clearer than last time, but still a bad connection.

"Hey, Ro! Sorry, the service here is bad. I'm ducked into a—" His words broke into incoherent syllables for a moment. "—love you, and I know we can make it through this." He paused, and I heard more noise in the background. "They're calling my—" More broken noise and dead air. "—call you later. Love you."

I frowned at the phone as the call cut off. I went to press 9 to save the message, but a bump at my arm made me hit the 7 instead.

"*Message deleted.*"

I cursed, looking up with a glare as a man rushed by me with a muttered "Excuse me" thrown over his shoulder.

I toyed with my phone for a moment, wishing there was an undo button. Finn had sounded kind of odd. I didn't know why I'd wanted to save the message, really. There was just something so unusual about it. The private number. The noise in the background. I checked the time of the incoming call, and it actually arrived *after* Finn's texts. So why was he calling when he'd already texted to tell me he was running late? And why was his number showing up on texts, but not on calls?

The day just kept getting stranger.

I got to Perk just as Finn pulled up to the curb, waving at me through the passenger window. I pulled the door open and tossed in my bag.

"Did you want coffee?" he asked, putting the car into park.

"God, no," I said with a laugh. "I need sleep more than caffeine, I think. This has been one weird day." I all but collapsed into the car, pulling the door shut behind me.

"Home, Phineas."

"Not my name," he said without missing a beat. He pulled smoothly into traffic. "My home or yours?" he asked with a smirk.

"Mine, please," I murmured, leaning my head back and closing my eyes. "I just want to go to bed."

"You okay?"

I hummed something in response. "Where were you when you called?" I asked, half-dozing already.

"Hmm?"

I opened my eyes to look at him drowsily. "I got your voicemail, but I couldn't really hear what you were saying."

He scanned the road before turning the corner leading to my apartment building. "Voicemail?"

I sat up, the queasy feeling in my stomach easing back in. "You said you had bad service. Said you loved me and we'd make it through this."

"Through what?"

"You tell me." I was getting irritated. What the hell was going on?

"Ro, I have no idea what you're talking about," he said, pulling to an abrupt stop in the parking lot of my apartment building. "I never left a voicemail. Not today."

I fumbled in my bag for my phone. I was not imagining this. "You did. You called—" I thumbed through my calls and held it up victoriously so he could see. "—at 12:06 p.m. today. See?"

His eyes narrowed at the screen. "That says *Private Number*."

Unscheduled Departure

"Yeah. Yeah, I know. I was going to ask you about that."

"Why do you think that was me?"

I rolled my eyes. "Because you left a voicemail!" My voice grew louder, a little screechy, but I couldn't help it.

"Babe, I never left you a voicemail today!" Finn said, aggravation growing in his own tone. He pulled out his own phone and stabbed at it a few times. Finn's familiar ringtone sounded on my phone, his picture popping up on the screen, along with his name.

"See?" he said. "At 12:06 I was driving. I didn't call you. Whoever that *Private Number* was, it wasn't me." He tapped his phone and the ringtone stopped.

I stared at my phone and rubbed my forehead. My stomach roiled and an ache throbbed behind my eyes. "I don't understand. I heard—"

"Let me listen to the voicemail."

"It...got deleted." I met Finn's unreadable gaze and knew how it sounded. Weird. Crazy. But I had heard him. It was Finn.

Wasn't it?

"I don't know what's happening," I murmured, my hands trembling as I brushed the hair away from my face. "I know what I heard."

"Ro," Finn reached across the car to grab my hand, wrapping it up in both of his. "It's okay."

"But—"

"We'll figure it out," he said, eyes wide and earnest. "I'm right here. We're together and we'll figure it out, I promise." He kissed my finger with a smile. "But after you sleep, okay?"

I forced a shaky smile. "Yeah. Okay."

"You want me to walk you up?" he asked.

I shook my head. Suddenly, I wanted to be alone. To go to sleep. To not think about all of this for a while. "I'll be fine. I'll call you later?"

"Okay." He leaned across the seat to kiss me. "Sleep well."

I nodded and got out of the car, waving at Finn and only letting my smile fall once he drove away.

I wasn't convinced. I knew what I had heard, and no matter what Finn said, it was him on that voice mail. I wondered if maybe the message was old— one I'd missed. I couldn't imagine how that might have happened, but I wasn't ruling it out just yet.

Because the alternative was one I wasn't quite ready to explore: If it was a new voice mail, and it was Finn who'd left it, that meant he was lying to me.

And I had no idea why.

3:22 PM

I blinked against the afternoon sunlight filtering through the gap in my bedroom curtains and stretched, surprised that I'd slept for so long. My stomach growled, reminding me that I'd skipped lunch, and I fumbled on the nightstand for my phone, hoping Lindsay would be up for an early dinner.

I scrolled through my texts, but she hadn't responded so I texted her again.

Starving and looking for an early dinner. Hitting the diner in 20. You in?

I rolled out of bed, figuring she'd join me if she was free and was just slipping on some shoes when my phone rang.

Private Number.

My stomach dropped and I hesitated, staring at the screen as the phone buzzed in my hand, the sound seeming to grow louder with every ring, echoing around the otherwise-silent room. The hair on the back of my neck stood on end, tingles racing down my spine as my thumb hovered over the answer button.

What was I doing? What was wrong with me? Afraid to answer my own phone?

It was ridiculous. I knew it was ridiculous, but I sat frozen for a long moment before I jolted, suddenly frantic, and pressed the call button with a trembling hand.

"Hello?" My voice was a cracked whisper. I cleared my throat and spoke a little louder. "Hello? Finn?"

"Hi, it's me . . . can you hear me?"

"Yeah. Yeah, I can hear you." I let out a soft laugh. "I can

Unscheduled Departure

believe I was so freaked out. I thought—"

"Rowan? Can you hear me?"

"I'm here. Finn?"

"Crap. This connection is terrible. Um. . . If you can hear me—"

"I can hear you!" My heart pounded. I wanted to reach out and touch him, frantic for some reason I couldn't put my finger on.

" —just wanted to let you know I'm here."

"Finn?"

"—wiped, so I'm going to try and get some sleep and I . . . uh . . guess I'll call you later. Maybe tomorrow, okay? Love you."

The call ended and I fumbled with the phone, hitting the call back button in desperate hope.

"Your call cannot be completed as dialed . . ."

A blend of fear and fury swept through me. What the hell was going on? With shaking fingers I scrolled through my contacts to Finn's number. Where was he calling me from? Why was he calling me? What was happening?

My phone buzzed with an incoming call and I jolted.

Lindsay.

I took a deep breath to calm my pounding heart and answered. "Linds?"

"Hey. Got your text. I can do dinner, but not at the diner, okay? You up for Chinese?"

"Um . . . yeah, yeah, sure. That sounds good."

"You sound kind of funny. Everything okay?" She paused, and I thought about how to answer, but she beat me to it. "Oh, crap. Finn left this morning, right? I can't believe I forgot."

This morning? Had it only been this morning? "No, it's not—"

"I had two midterms today and I just— I'm so sorry Ro."

"It's okay, Linds. He didn't go."

I heard a noise over the phone, could picture Lindsay stopping in the middle of the sidewalk, mouth dropped open in shock. "He what?"

"Changed his mind." I shrugged, even though I knew she

couldn't see it. "He said he didn't want to leave me."

Lindsay laughed, full-bodied and loud. "Well, the guy sure has the romantic hero thing down. It's like a friggin' Kate Hudson movie."

I snorted.

"So, you're okay then?" she asked, tentative.

"Yeah." I didn't even convince myself.

"Ro?"

I sighed. "I don't know, Linds. Something's up with Finn. I don't know if I'm imagining it or what, but . . ."

"But what?"

And that was the rub. I had no idea.

"That settles it," Lindsay said after I'd been quiet for too long. "I'm picking up takeout and I'll be there in twenty minutes. We're going to eat Chinese and have girl talk and—I don't know, hell, bake cookies and do our nails or something."

"Girl talk?"

"Shut up. I can totally do girl talk," she said. "I'll girl talk the heck out of you and we'll figure out all your boy troubles."

"I don't have—"

"Twenty minutes." Lindsay hung up and I closed my mouth when I realized it was still hanging open. Lindsay was a force of nature, but she was also a good friend and maybe . . . maybe I needed to talk to someone about the whole Finn-weirdness that was going on. Someone who'd assure me that I wasn't crazy, but who could give me a rational explanation for everything that had happened.

Someone who could give me a reason that didn't include Finn lying to me.

Finn.

I thumbed through my contacts to his name again, and didn't hesitate to press the call button.

He answered on the second ring. "Hey."

"Hey." I swallowed, nervous, although I knew I shouldn't be. "I, uh. Got your call?"

"Hmm?" He seemed distracted.

"Finn?"

Unscheduled Departure

He cleared his throat. "Sorry. Working on a letter to the admissions office. I'm hoping I'll be able to come back next quarter." I heard a couple of clicks, probably his computer keyboard. "What did you say?"

"Um . . . nothing, really. I just got your call, and . . . I thought you were tired?" My heart thumped in my chest, palms sweaty as I waited for his response.

"Kind of," he replied. "But I really wanted to get this letter off. I'm supposed to meet the guys for din—"

"But you're tired. You said you were wiped." I felt my voice rising with my agitation.

"What are you talking about? I'm not that tired."

"You called me. From the private number—"

"Ro—"

"The connection was bad, but you said you were tired. You said you'd call me tomorrow." I forced the words out, even and firm. He had to remember. He had to. "You said you loved me."

"Ro, I told you that wasn't me. I didn't call you."

"Not this morning," I snapped. "Just now. You called me just now!"

"It wasn't me. I swear, Ro, I've been working on this letter for an hour." He sounded worried, his voice soothing, like he was . . . like he was talking down a crazy person. "Babe, are you okay?"

"I—" I twisted my fingers in my hair. "But you did. I heard you."

"I'm coming over."

"No!" Panic seized me. I didn't know why, but I needed to figure this out myself. If Finn were there, I'd only get more confused. "No, it's okay," I said, forcing myself to sound calm, even. "It's probably some kids playing a prank or something."

"I can tell the guys I'm busy."

"No, Finn, it's fine, really." I laughed, the sound harsh and tinny to my own ears. "Lindsay's coming over for a girl's night. We're going to hang out and watch a movie or something."

Finn was silent for a moment. "You sure?"

"Yeah, yeah, of course. Like I said, it's probably just a stupid prank."

"Well, if they call back, you should call the cops or something. They can trace it and get the little monsters to leave you alone."

I let out another short laugh. "Well, I don't think it'll come to that. I'll just ignore the calls from now on."

"Good idea." I heard a rustle of fabric. "You sure you're okay?"

I let out a quiet breath.

No.

"I'm fine," I said. "Have fun tonight and I'll talk to you tomorrow?"

"Yeah, okay. Love you."

I swallowed, a dry gulp, and my words came out choked. "Love you, too."

I hung up and set the phone down next to me on the bed. I'd lied to Finn. Lied when I said I was fine. Lied when I said I thought the calls were a prank.

Because I knew they weren't. I knew Finn's voice and—bad connection or not—I'd recognize it anywhere. It *had* been Finn who called me. But I also couldn't believe he'd lie to me about it. Couldn't understand why he would.

I was still sitting there, my mind on an endless loop, when a knock sounded at my front door. I got up to answer it, leaving the phone behind, and found Lindsay standing in the hall, tapping her foot impatiently.

"They were out of pancakes for the Moo Shu, so we'll just have to make do," she said as she pushed by me, plastic bags dangling from her fingers. Her colorful skirt swirled around her, the familiar scent of patchouli oil wafting in her wake.

"I brought wine," she said as she set the bags on the kitchen table. "Where's your corkscrew?"

"Top drawer."

"Sit," she ordered, jerking her head toward the couch.

"Linds, I'm fine."

Her eyes narrowed and she took two steps toward me. "Your aura's all muddy, brown at the edges. You are not all

Unscheduled Departure

right." She waved her hands as if to encompass all my not-all-rightness, then pointed to the couch. "Sit. I'm pouring wine. We're eating. Then you're going to tell me what's going on."

With a heavy sigh, I flopped onto the couch, my head dropping back into the soft cushions as I closed my eyes. Lindsay pressed a glass into my hand and I took an obedient sip of wine before digging into the plate she set before me.

I ate on autopilot, feeling Lindsay's concerned eyes on me. True to her word, though, she kept the conversation light— talking about classes and her job at a New Age book store— until I pushed my empty plate away and swallowed the last of my wine.

"Okay," she said, waving her hands in a "come on" gesture. "Spill."

I collapsed back against the couch and rubbed my hands over my face. "I don't know where to start."

"Start with Finn."

I glanced at her from between my fingers. Sometimes I thought Lindsay was a little bit flaky, despite the fact that she was my best friend. Other times, she was startlingly intuitive. I sighed.

"There's something . . . wrong with Finn."

She leaned forward, elbows on her knees. "Wrong how?"

I threw up my hands. "I don't know. That's the problem."

"Okay . . . okay." She got up and moved beside me on the couch, grabbing my hand. "Take a breath and clear your mind, and then tell me what you mean."

I closed my eyes and took a deep breath, my mind flitting over the events of the day.

"I'm not sure exactly what it is," I said, finally. "There's just been all this strange stuff happening today. I mean, maybe it's nothing and I'm just imagining things." I glanced at Lindsay and she nodded in encouragement.

"Okay," I said. "It started this morning, after we got back from the airport." I told her about the phone calls, showed her the *Private Number* in my call history.

She examined the phone then handed back. "And you're sure it was Finn."

"I know his voice, Linds. It was him."

Lindsay frowned. "But why? Why would he call you from some blocked number and then say he didn't?"

I collapsed in on myself, clutching my arms across the growing queasiness in my stomach. "I don't know. It doesn't make any sense. I know it sounds crazy—"

"You are *not* crazy," she said firmly. And that pretty much summed up our friendship. No matter what, Lindsay had my back.

"There's more," I said slowly. "Finn seems . . . weird. Off, somehow. Different. I can't explain it. I keep thinking I'm imagining things— it's Finn, you know?"

Lindsay nodded, although I was sure she had no idea.

"But then, a couple of times today . . . " I considered my words carefully. "He'd do something or say something and it just seemed like he was . . . different. It was like he wasn't . . . " I swallowed. "Finn."

Lindsay's eyes widened. "Okay, that's just creepy."

"I know—"

"Like some *Invasion of the Body Snatchers*, *Exorcist* kind of stuff." She shuddered.

"I know!" I stood up and crossed to the window, turned and paced back. "I know how it sounds, and I can't explain it. But I know Finn, and something is wrong, Linds. I don't know what it is, but something's wrong."

She shot to her feet and pulled me into a hug. "It's okay," she said quietly as I let out a shaky breath. "We're going to figure this out."

I pulled back to look into her eyes. "How?"

"Maybe you should talk to him."

"I tried," I said.

"Maybe you should try again."

I turned away, tugging at my hair. "I . . . don't think that'll help, Linds. I really don't."

She was quiet and when I looked back at her, she frowned and nodded. "Okay, then. I think I need to see Finn."

"You think that'll help?"

She shrugged. "Well, it couldn't hurt. Maybe I'll get a read on him and it'll help us get some answers."

"You going to read his aura?"

Lindsay glared at me. "I know you think it's BS, but you have to admit I'm right more than I'm wrong."

I sighed. "Yeah. Okay. But isn't he going to think it's weird?"

"Sheesh, Ro, I'm not going to walk up to the guy and ask him if he's an alien. What do you take me for? I can be discreet."

I raised a disbelieving brow.

"I can!" she protested. "I went this whole time without telling you you look like crap, didn't I?"

I burst out laughing, suddenly feeling not quite so alone.

6:03 PM

"I'm not so sure about this," I told Lindsay as we peered through the window into the pizza place. "I feel like a stalker."

Lindsay gripped my arm and pulled me flat against the brick wall. "Try and act casual. We just happened to want pizza. Finn just happened to be here."

I gave her an unimpressed look. "It's where he and his friends always go. He's going to know it's not a coincidence."

She rolled her eyes. "Then, you missed him and wanted to see him. He's your boyfriend, Ro. It's not unheard of. Come on, work with me here."

I nodded. Reluctantly. "Can you see him? Can you tell anything from here?"

Lindsay turned to look through the window. "No, not really. They're all the way in the back. We need to go in."

I sighed heavily. "Okay. But we just stopped in to say hi on the way to the movies. We're not staying. I'm not the weirdo stalker girlfriend."

"That's the spirit." Lindsay bumped my shoulder and I followed her through the glass door into the restaurant's dim interior.

The scent of garlic and spices enveloped me as we made our way to the back of the restaurant, where Finn and his friends stood around one of the pool tables. A couple of large pizzas and half-empty pitchers of beer sat on the counter that ran along the wall, and Finn leaned his cue against one of the stools so he could grab a slice and take a large bite. He spotted me and started to smile, then apparently realized how gross that would be with a mouthful of pepperoni. He set down the rest of his pizza and swallowed before leaning down to kiss me.

"Hey," he said, nodding at Lindsay. "What are you guys doing here?"

"Heading to a movie and we just stopped in to say hello. We're not staying," Lindsay said quickly.

Discreet. *Right*.

"Okay," Finn said slowly. "You want some pizza?"

"No," I replied, smiling at him. "Really, we were just passing by."

"Are you sure . . .?" Finn glanced up at Lindsay, then pulled me aside, lowering his voice. "Are you sure you're okay? You sounded really upset on the phone."

I forced myself to smile wider. "Yeah, I'm fine. Really."

"How are you, Finn?" Lindsay asked, eyeing him closely. "You feeling okay?"

"Uh, yeah." Finn glanced at me sideways. He generally thought Lindsay was weird. This wasn't helping.

"No blackouts?" she asked. "Memory loss? Finding yourself someplace without realizing how you got there?"

"Lindsay," I groaned.

"What is this about?" Finn asked, and I heard the edge of irritation in his voice.

"Nothing!" I grabbed Lindsay to pull her from the room. "We've got to go if we're going to make the movie on time."

"But—"

"Linds," I muttered. "Let's. Go." I waved at Finn. "Talk to you tomorrow, okay?"

Finn lifted a hand to wave back, and he looked more than a little dazed. I couldn't say I blamed him.

When we got out onto the sidewalk, I kept walking until we were out of sight of the pizza place, then sat on a bench outside a small cafe. Lindsey sat down next to me and gave me a sheepish grin.

Unscheduled Departure

"Discreet, huh?" I poked her shoulder.

"Hey— I tried," she exclaimed. "But I wasn't getting anything, so I thought maybe if I prodded him a little, got a response . . ."

"And?"

"And . . ." she sighed. "And nothing."

"Nothing?"

She shook her head. "He looks the same to me. His aura's blue with a little purple and green— like always. I didn't see anything out of the ordinary. Sorry."

I slumped. "No, it's okay." I wasn't sure what I expected. What I wanted. "Maybe I *am* imagining all of this."

Lindsay nudged me with her shoulder and somehow it was comforting. We sat in silence for a while, lost in our own thoughts, then Lindsay nudged me again.

"Maybe we need to look at this logically, methodically," she said.

"What do you mean?"

"You know what they say. When you have eliminated the impossible, whatever remains, however improbable, must be the truth." Lindsay nodded sagely.

"Oh my god, are you quoting Sherlock Holmes to me?"

She blinked. "That was Mr. Spock."

"Pretty sure Spock was quoting Sherlock Holmes."

"Whatever." She waved a hand, a wave of patchouli hitting me with the movement. "The point is, we need to look at this like Spock, or *Sherlock*— " She gave me an indulgent nod. "—would. Logically. Methodically. We go through all this weird stuff that's been going on, make a list of possible explanations, eliminate the impossible. And whatever's left. . ." She shrugged.

"Must be the truth," I murmured.

"That's what I'm saying." She fumbled in her bag and pulled out an old receipt and a pen. "So, we have the phone calls, and you said he seems different," she said, scribbling on the paper. "How do you mean? Can you be more specific?"

I chewed on my lip. "His hair looks different. I don't know how that could be, but I think it's shorter maybe?"

Lindsay frowned, but added it to the list. "Tell me about

the calls," she said. "What exactly did he say?"

"Let me think," I replied. "Okay, the first time—"

"What time was that?"

"Ummm . . ." I pulled out my phone and thumbed through the received call. "The first call was at 9:57. Then 12:06. Last one at . . . 3:25."

Lindsay wrote it all down. "Okay— what did he say the first time? Try to remember exactly, if you can."

I searched my memory. "Not much, really. At least not much I could understand. The connection was really bad and it kept cutting out." I thought for a moment. "There was noise in the background. I remember thinking it was a loudspeaker, maybe? But that doesn't make any sense."

"Loudspeaker. Okay," Lindsay said. "Then what?"

"Next was the voice mail I accidentally deleted," I replied, still frustrated by that fact. "He said he loved me and that we could make it through this."

Lindsay sat up a little. "Through what?"

"I don't know."

She hummed. "Anything else?"

I shrugged. "It was a bad connection again. He said the service was bad wherever he was. Right before he hung up he said, 'They're calling my...' something. I couldn't make it out."

Lindsay sat back and stared out across the street, pondering that. "Calling my name? Calling my number? Maybe he was at a bank?"

"Or a post office. Or a deli. Or the doctor's office." I threw up my hands. "This isn't getting us anywhere."

"Don't give up now," she said, turning back to her list. "What about the last call?"

I narrowed my eyes as I tried to focus on that call, Finn's voice. "It was a bad connection again."

"Seems to be a theme." I glanced at her and she shrugged. "It might be important. He must have been in a bad coverage area. We're not ruling anything out, right?"

I nodded. "Okay. So, yeah, it was a bad connection, and I could hear him, but he couldn't hear me. Umm, he said he was tired and was going to get some sleep and he'd call me tomorrow."

Unscheduled Departure

"But we just saw him. He didn't seem tired at all."

"That's what I'm saying! Ugh!" I threw up my hands.

"Okay, okay." Lindsay tapped the pen against her lips. "Anything else?"

"I don't think so," I replied. "He asked if I could hear him. I said I could, but he couldn't hear me. Then he said . . ." I closed my eyes and tilted my head back as I remembered his words. "He said, 'If you can hear me, I just wanted to let you know I'm here.'"

"I'm here?" Lindsay murmured. "Like— 'I'm here for you' kind of here?"

"No. I think . . . " I said slowly, rolling the words around in my mouth, in my mind, before speaking them out loud. "That's not how he said it. It was more like . . . like 'I've arrived.'"

"Arrived where?"

"I have no idea."

"So . . ." Lindsay doodled on a corner of the paper, thinking for a moment. "I'm here. I love you. We can make it through this. It's almost like—" She sat up a little. "You're sure these calls all came in after Finn had decided not to go home?"

"Well, yeah. I mean, according to my phone."

Lindsay held up a finger. "So, theory number one: Your phone is screwed up. Or the calls were delayed? Maybe he placed them earlier, before he changed his mind about leaving?"

"But only those particular calls were delayed?" I asked. "And Finn already said he never made the calls."

"So theory number two: the calls were from someone else."

"Someone who called me by name? Told me he loved me?"

"Okay, strike theory number two," Lindsay said. She eyed me nervously. "Which brings us to theory number three."

I knew where she was going. I didn't like it, but it wasn't like I hadn't thought about it myself. "You think Finn's lying."

"I don't think anything. I'm simply throwing out

theories."

"Yeah, well, I don't like that one." I let out a heavy breath, air hissing between my clenched teeth. "But I have to admit it's possible. The question is, *Why*?"

Lindsay thought about that. "I don't know. Why would a guy who's basically choosing you over his family make a bunch of weird phone calls, and then say he didn't?"

"It doesn't make sense. None of this does."

Lindsay folded up the list and put it in her bag. "Well, there's only one thing to do, really."

"What?"

"Finn said he'd call again, right?"

"Yeah," I replied slowly. "Tomorrow."

"You need to let that call go to voicemail. Get a recording of it so you have some proof. Then you can confront him with it."

The thought made my stomach churn. "That feels kind of . . ."

"Brilliant?" she offered.

"I was thinking more like sneaky."

Lindsay huffed. "Look, Ro. If it really is Finn making these calls, and he is lying to you, there's only one way to find out. I mean, what's the alternative?"

"I don't know," I said, rubbing my eyes. "I just can't imagine why he would do something like that."

"Well, what other explanation is there?"

"There has to be one," I said, getting to my feet. "We just haven't figured it out yet."

"Okay, fine," Lindsay said, catching up to me as I headed down the street. "But it won't hurt anything to record the call, right? If anything, it'll help prove that it's *not* Finn. Then you can solve this together." She held out her hands, palms up, and smiled innocently. Hopefully.

Deceitfully. I didn't buy it for a second.

But she had a point. At least I'd have proof that it wasn't all in my head - that I wasn't imagining it.

Or maybe, I thought nervously, it would prove exactly that.

Unscheduled Departure

6:06 AM
Wednesday

My phone didn't wake me the next morning. It would have. I chose the most annoying ringtone I could find and cranked up the volume, terrified that I'd sleep through the next call from Fi— the next call from *Private Number*. Lindsay wanted to stay with me, but I fought her on that and won. She had an early-morning exam and I didn't need or want a babysitter.

I could do this on my own.

Fortunately, I didn't have a midterm until Friday, and it was in my Intro to World Religions class, which had been a piece of cake so far. There was no way I could have studied anyway. So Lindsay stuck around for a while and watched bad reality TV with me, and we ate popcorn and ice cream until I felt like I'd burst. She didn't leave until I promised her I was tired enough to sleep, and that I'd call her as soon as I heard from Finn. Or whoever.

But in the end, my phone didn't wake me because I hardly slept that night. Instead, I tossed and turned, moments of fitful dozing interspersed with hours of staring at the ceiling. I was mid-stare when the Macarena jolted me out of a daze, and I shot up into a sitting position, reaching for the phone at the same time.

But no. It had to go to voicemail.

It seemed like forever that I sat there staring at the screen, the words *Private Number* mocking me, and the electronic music harsh and grating in the silence. Everything in me ached to answer, to try again, but I knew Lindsay was right. I couldn't answer. Not this time.

So I waited until the music cut out and the little voicemail icon popped onto the screen. Then, with trembling fingers, I pressed it.

"*You have one unheard message.*"

I held my breath, waiting.

"Hi, it's me . . . "

Before I heard another word, I forced myself to let out my breath slowly, calmly, and press the 9 button.

"*Message saved.*"

Proof.

I replayed the message and put the phone on speaker, feeling a need to look at the screen as the message played back, as if watching the display somehow linked me more solidly to Finn. He sounded far away again, the call filled with extraneous noises, but I could still make out his words.

"Hi, it's me . . . oh, sorry, you must be sleeping. I forgot it's still early there."

I glanced at the clock to see it was just after six.

"Anyway, I'll be in meetings all morning, so if you call and I don't answer, that's why. I'll, uh, call when we get a break for lunch, okay? I really want to hear your voice." I heard a shuffling in the background, an intake of breath as if he was going to say something more. "Okay, then. Love you."

A click as the call ended, then, "*You have no more saved messages.*"

I played it again . . . and again. Listening to the rising and falling tones, the structure of his words— searching for anything, any clue that would tell me it wasn't Finn.

But I couldn't find one.

With each passing second, each time re-playing the message, I only became more and more certain that it was Finn's voice on the phone. And while that answered one question, it only raised a thousand more.

Why?

Why did he insist he never called? That it wasn't him? Was something wrong with him? Was he calling me in his sleep or under some kind of hypnosis?

If not, why would he lie?

I wanted to call him. No, really, I wanted to see him. Play the message and watch his response when he heard his own unmistakable voice on the crackling connection. I was already on my feet and reaching for my keys when Finn's words registered.

". . . forgot it's still early there. . . meetings all morning . . . when we break for lunch . . ."

What was he talking about? He'd told me about trying to get back in school for the next quarter, but why would he be in meetings all morning? And how could he forget it's early here?

I was missing something — something huge that tickled at the edge of my consciousness, but I couldn't figure out what it was. Words and ideas flitted through my mind, theories created and discarded, and I found myself scribbling in a notebook, creating a more detailed list than the one on the back of Lindsay's receipt.

I stared at the ink-filled page, neat columns marred by arrows pointing left and right, and reached for my phone to text Lindsay.

Coffee after your class?

The response was almost immediate.

Absolutely. Done at 9. See you then.

Then, barely a second later.

Did he call? Are you okay?

Was I? I took a shaky breath.

I'm fine. Just not sure what to do now.

I had to laugh at the next text.

I suggest a shower. See you at 9.

And since I had a few hours to kill, and nothing else to do but worry, I followed Lindsay's advice.

9:11 AM

I was on my second latte— which probably wasn't the best choice, given my current state of mind— when Lindsay blew through the coffee shop door and spotted me at our usual table in the back. The place was all but empty, a guy on a computer by the front door and the barista behind the counter our only company. Lindsay slid into the seat across from me, concern evident all over her face.

"How was your midterm?" I asked, tapping out a rhythm on my coffee cup with jittery fingers.

She waved away my question with an impatient frown. "Come on," she said. "Spill."

I let out a heavy breath and spun my phone on the table, letting it slow before I picked it up to dial into voicemail and switch on the speakerphone. I watched Lindsay with bated breath as the message played back.

"Hi, it's me . . . " I chewed on my thumbnail and focused on Lindsay as she stared, forehead creased in concentration, at the phone lying on the table. She jumped when the automated voice kicked in and looked up at me.

"I don't understand," she said slowly.

"I know it's kind of a bad connection," I replied, thumbing at the phone. "Listen again."

"Ro—"

"No, shh," I said as the message started again. "Listen."

Lindsay sat obediently, watching me this time, instead of the phone. She continued to stare as the message ended and I disconnected the call. I didn't know what she was waiting for, why she was so quiet.

"Well?" I kind of snapped, impatient and on edge.

"Well what, Ro?" Lindsay said quietly. Too quietly.

Unease prickled up my spine at her confused, concerned expression. "You don't think it's him," I said, already knowing the answer.

At least I thought I did.

"You . . . " Lindsay swallowed. "You think Finn left that message?"

"Well, yeah. Of course I do," I replied, anxiety knotting in my stomach. "I know it's kind of hard to hear him—"

"You hear him?" She reached across the table and grabbed my hand, stilling my unconscious fidgeting. "What did he say?"

I stared at her blankly for a moment. "What do you mean? You heard him. He said—"

"Ro." She squeezed my hand. "I didn't hear him."

"But—" That couldn't be right. "Of course you did. It's not that loud in here."

She shook her head, eyes soft and sad. "I didn't, Ro. All I heard was some static."

"No. No, listen." I fumbled for the phone, switched it off speaker and dialed into voicemail again. "Put it against your ear this time."

"Ro—"

"Just do it!" I thrust the phone at her, oblivious to the

Unscheduled Departure

others around us. "Please."

Lindsay took the phone and held it to her ear. I could hear Finn's voice even across the table, and I watched for her reaction, my heart racing. She had to hear it. She had to.

But after a moment she just slid the phone across the table. "I'm sorry, Ro."

"Nothing?" I whispered.

She shook her head.

"I . . . I don't understand," I said, my eyes still focused on the phone long after the screen went black. "No. No, it's him. I know it is." I shot to my feet and grabbed the phone, searching the coffee shop frantically until my gaze focused on the barista behind the counter.

"Ro, wait," Lindsay said, getting to her feet.

"No, I heard it. I know I did." I hurried to the counter, dialing along the way. "Excuse me," I said to the barista. "I need your help."

He smiled and reached for a cup. "Sure, another latte?"

"No, no more coffee. That's the last thing I need," I said with a forced laugh. At his confused expression, I held out the phone. "Would you listen to this voicemail please?"

He blinked. "You want me to—"

"Ro—" Lindsay reached for me, but I shook off her hand.

"Please," I said to the barista, not even embarrassed that I sounded so desperate.

Lindsay stepped up beside me, smiling. "It's a bet," she said. "I've got ten bucks on it. Could you just tell us what you hear?"

The barista looked back and forth between us, then shrugged and reached for the phone. I pressed the replay button and he held it to his ear, pursing his lips as he listened. After a moment, he handed it back to me.

"Some static," he said. "You got a crank caller?"

My heart sank. "You didn't hear anything else?"

He took a step back, probably because of my crazy eyes. Or my crazy face. Or my whole crazy demeanor.

"Not really." He turned to wait on a customer and I resisted the urge to ask him to listen again.

Lindsay took my arm gently and led me back to the table.

I sank back into my chair, confusion and fear bringing tears to my eyes.

"Am I . . . am I losing it, Linds?"

To her credit, Lindsay didn't rush to reassure me, but looked at me closely, her eyes narrowed in concentration. "No," she said softly. Then, a little firmer. "No. You're not losing it. But something strange is going on here."

I exhaled a snorted laugh and brushed away my tears. "Yeah. That's putting it mildly."

"Okay, we need to focus," Lindsay said, reaching into her bag to pull out a pen. "Tell me what he said."

"Here." I produced my own notebook, flipping it open to my scratched out columns. Lindsay smiled tightly and clicked her pen to the ready.

I didn't even have to think this time. I'd heard the message so many times it was etched into my memory. I recited it to her with the same pauses and inflections, and described the noises in the background. Lindsay wrote it down word-for-word, then sat examining the page, the pen caught tight between her teeth.

"It's like . . . " She underlined a few words. "It's like he's calling from somewhere far away."

I gasped— not from shock, not really— but because she'd put voice to my own thoughts. "But he's here," I protested. "He lives ten minutes from here."

"Maybe . . . " Lindsay looked off over my shoulder, lost in thought.

"What is it?" I asked.

Lindsay's gaze focused on mine and she worked her jaw. I knew that look. It was the same look she had right before she said something about my aura or mentioned her sixth sense. The look that said she knew I didn't totally believe her, but that I would listen.

It was ironic that she wasn't the only one feeling like that lately.

"Tell me," I said.

"I think . . . what if? What if you've found a . . . *portal* of some kind?"

"Portal? Portal to what, exactly?"

Unscheduled Departure

Lindsay shrugged. "The spirit realm? Another dimension? I don't know."

My first instinct was to laugh. It spoke to my desperation that I clung to her words, though. I needed to believe there was an answer beyond that I was imagining things.

"You think I'm getting phone calls from Finn's spirit?" I asked, a chill running down my spine. "But . . . I mean, wouldn't he have to be dead for that?"

Lindsay sat back and laced her fingers together— her teaching pose. "You're thinking too linearly," she said, drawing a straight line with her finger in the air. "There is no time on the other side."

"So, you're saying, what? It's Finn's ghost, from the future?" It all sounded so ridiculous. But then again, so did getting voice mails that only I could hear.

"Or perhaps another Finn."

Okay, what? "Okay, what?"

Lindsay smirked. "It's kind of arrogant to think we're all there is, you know? There are theories of other dimensions, other universes or realities. Some that are very similar to our own. Maybe, somehow, you've been communicating with a Finn in one of those other realities."

I slumped back in my seat. "Come on, you don't really believe that, do you?"

"How else would you explain it?" She raised a brow in challenge and lifted a finger. "You're sure it's Finn on the phone. You don't think Finn— the Finn here and now— is lying about not calling you." She ticked off the items on her fingers. "The Finn on the phone seems to be calling from far away. And apparently only you can hear him." Lindsay leaned forward, elbows on the table. "Face it, Ro. You've opened a portal to another realm or something."

"Through my phone," I said flatly. "I can barely get service in Costco and you're telling me it's getting calls from another dimension?"

Lindsay just shrugged. "Don't make me quote Spock again."

"Sherlock."

"Whatever." She grabbed my hands across the table. "The

point is, something is happening to you. And, like it or not, it seems to be something not of this world." She waved her hands wiggling her fingers to emphasize her words, then picked up her pen and tapped it on the list. I knew she was waiting. Waiting for me to respond, to acknowledge what she'd said.

To believe.

I wasn't quite there yet.

"Okay, let's say you're right." At her victorious look, I hurried to add, "Not that I'm saying you are, but hypothetically speaking." I waited until she nodded slightly.

"How would it happen? And why? Am I supposed to, I don't know, do something?"

She frowned. "Like what?"

"I don't know." I threw up my hands and sat back. "But I would assume things like this happen for a reason. And if I've created some kind of portal, couldn't it cause a tear in space-time or something?"

Lindsay snorted. "Now who's quoting Spock?"

"Okay, touché," I said, rolling my eyes. "But you're the one who's so big on destiny and fate and . . . and karma and everything. Shouldn't there be a reason for all of this?"

Lindsay pondered that for a moment. "Yes, I would think so. It would seem Finn— the Finn on the phone— has a message for you. He has to be trying to tell you something."

"Tell me what, though?" I asked, more than a little exasperated. "He hasn't been saying anything significant."

Lindsay visibly deflated. "I don't know."

I reached for the notebook and flipped it around to study the list. "It's all outrageous anyway," I muttered. "Alternate realities and portals." I scanned the page before me.

I forgot it's early there.
We can make it through this.
"There's got to be some other explanation," I said.
The coffee stain - when did he change his shirt?
"Got to be . . . "
He's different. Something's different.
...meetings all morning...
Different

...it's early there.

"Ro?" Lindsay's voice jolted me out of my thoughts.

"What is it?" she asked.

I looked down at the notebook again, the pieces beginning to fit together in a strange, outlandish puzzle.

"These alternate dimensions or whatever," I said slowly. "If people can communicate between them . . ."

"Yeah?"

"Could they actually . . . God, this sounds so crazy." I slumped back and hid my face in my hands.

Lindsay reached across the table to pull my hands away. "Not crazy, Ro. What are you thinking? Tell me."

"Okay." I took a breath and went for broke. "Could someone actually travel between these realities?"

She frowned in concentration for a moment. "I'm no expert, Ro. But . . . yeah. From what I've read, it's theoretically possible with the right focus and if the veil between the realities is thin enough."

I couldn't be bothered with the details. Not when the words on the page before me were swimming, my head spinning.

"What is it, Ro?"

"What if . . ." My words came out as a croak, so I cleared my throat, bracing myself. "What if it's not what Finn's saying on the phone, but just that he's speaking to me at all?"

"What do you mean?"

"Since this started, I've had this feeling that things are . . . off. Wrong. With Finn, I mean."

She nodded slowly.

"What if Finn didn't change his mind about going to Virginia?" I whispered.

Lindsay's eyes widened. "You mean—"

"What if Finn— my Finn— actually went? And he's calling me from there."

I forgot it's still early there.
Meetings all morning.
We'll make it through this.
Love you.

"But if that's true." Lindsay lowered her voice and

glanced over her shoulder. I wasn't sure why. There was nobody else nearby. "That means the Finn who's here isn't *your* Finn."

"Could that really happen?" I asked. "Could they switch places somehow, and my Finn is able to reach out to me . . . because I'm supposed to fix it somehow?"

Lindsay looked a little lost. I didn't blame her.

"I don't know, Ro," she said finally. "But I think we have to find out. I'm just not sure how."

I sighed and scanned the list one more time. "I think I might have an idea."

11:47 AM

"Are you sure about this?" Lindsay asked, glancing down the hall nervously.

I slipped my key into Finn's front door. "I have to know," I replied.

"Maybe you should just ask him?"

I froze and bowed my head, bumping it against the door. "Maybe I should," I said quietly. "But if I'm wrong, I can't—I don't want him to know about all of this. And if I'm right . . . "

The thought was overwhelming. What would I do if I was right? I had no idea.

Lindsay pressed a hand to my back. "Okay then, let's go."

We slipped into Finn's apartment and I called out to make sure he was really gone. He'd texted that he was heading over to talk to the dean about readmission, and we'd agreed to meet for lunch afterward. Part of me felt guilty sneaking around in his home. The other part of me —the desperate and terrified part— was pretty sure I didn't have any other option.

"Where do we look?" Lindsay asked, taking in the unpacked boxes and stacks of books on the floor.

"Bedroom first." I led her down the hallway and into the room. It was small, like most student housing, with a full bed in one corner and a dresser crammed in the other, the right side jutting into the closet opening a couple of inches. A small desk and bookshelf took up the rest of the room, with a glass door leading to a small balcony bringing in some natural

Unscheduled Departure

light. He'd unpacked this room, the empty boxes folded neatly and stacked behind the door.

I headed straight for the closet and flipped on the light. I grabbed the small clothes hamper tucked behind the door and dumped it on the floor.

"What are we looking for?" Lindsay asked as I picked through the dirty laundry.

"White button down," I replied, "with a coffee stain on the sleeve. He has another hamper in the bathroom. Can you check there?"

She nodded and disappeared out the door, only to return a few seconds later. "Only a towel in that one," she said. "Any luck?"

I picked up a blue shirt, and threw it back down. "No, it's not here."

"Maybe he washed it already?" Lindsay suggested, hesitating as she reached for a dresser drawer.

"I'll look in there. You check the closet?"

We went to work, Lindsay holding up a shirt every now and then for me to review. With each moment that passed, my heart sank further into my stomach.

"It's no use," I said, not even bothering to close the bottom drawer. "It's not here."

"What's not here?" a familiar voice said from the doorway.

I turned to see Finn looking at us with a baffled expression, taking in the mess on the floor, the open drawers, and the two women apparently searching his bedroom.

Well, no apparently about it.

"Ro? What are you doing?" he asked.

"Uh—" I looked to Lindsay, but she was just as stunned as I was. "I thought you were meeting with the dean?"

"He had a family emergency and had to reschedule," he said. "Ro, what's going on here?"

I cleared my throat. "I was, uh, looking for your shirt."

"My shirt? What shirt?"

"The one you were wearing the other morning. The one you spilled coffee on."

He stood there for a moment, gaping, before his gaze

cleared and anger replaced the surprise. "You're still going on about that?"

I took a step toward him. "Finn, no. Please listen—"

"To what?" he snapped, stalking to the pile of dirty laundry and stuffing it back into the hamper. "You're going through my dirty laundry, Rowan. You don't think that's a little—"

"Little what? Insane?" I snapped.

"I didn't say that!"

"You didn't have to!"

We glared at each other and Lindsay chose that moment to step forward. "Ro—"

"It's okay," I said, swallowing my nerves. "Could you give us a minute?"

She glanced nervously at Finn. "You sure?"

"Yeah."

"Okay. I'm, uh, going to . . . " She jerked a thumb toward the door. "Call me later?"

I nodded.

She murmured a quiet apology as she passed Finn, but he either didn't hear it, or chose to ignore it. When the front door shut quietly behind her, Finn let out a heavy breath.

"What's going on with you?" he asked, anger dissipating as he sat down on the bed. He lifted a hand, as if to reach out to me, but let it fall back into his lap. "Talk to me."

And in that moment, I knew I had only one option. I had to tell Finn the truth. Because he was Finn. Whether or not he was *my* Finn was irrelevant, because even if he was from some other reality— I still couldn't believe the thought— he had his own Rowan. His own me. We were together, and we loved each other— trusted each other— and I had to honor that, no matter what.

I sat down beside him and turned sideways so I could meet his gaze. "I'm going to tell you something that sounds insane," I said. "But I need you to trust me and I need you to keep an open mind."

His eyes darted back and forth, searching my own, then he picked up my hand, lifted it to his lips, and kissed my finger.

Unscheduled Departure

"Tell me," he said.

All in all, it went better than I thought it would. He wasn't convinced— I mean, who would be, besides maybe Lindsay— but he didn't call me crazy, and he didn't try to debunk my theory. He just listened, asked a few questions, frowned when I told him about the other Finn saying he loved me, and held my hand the whole time. Then he sat, staring at the pile of dirty laundry in the middle of the floor, until I was about out of my mind.

"Well?" I asked, when I couldn't stand it anymore.

"I don't know what you want me to say."

"You can say you believe me."

"It's not about believing you, Ro," he said quietly. "It's just a lot to take in. That you don't think I'm . . . me."

"You're you. You're just not—" I got to my feet, an idea starting to form. "Think about it," I said. "Doesn't anything seem strange to you, different since we got back from the airport? Am I different?"

He looked up at me, tension at the corners of his eyes as he studied me. I latched on to that doubt— that curiosity.

"It might be something little, insignificant," I said, falling to my knees before him. "Maybe my hair's a little off, or my voice is weird?"

Finn licked his lips. "You . . . you called me Finnester."

"Yeah? I always do that." My little annoying nick-names for Finn were kind of a tradition. "Don't I?"

"Yeah, yeah, you do," he said, rubbing his hands over his face. "But you'd called me that particular name before— at the house just that morning— you never re-use your names, at least not so close together."

"What?" I sat back on my heels, trying to remember. "Are you sure?" I did try to mix it up, and come up with different variations— just to drive Finn crazy, or make him laugh.

"And your fingernails," he murmured, bringing my hand to his face. "They were pink. Did you take off the polish?" He looked up at me, a growing shock showing in his expression. I knew how he felt.

"No," I whispered. "I haven't worn nail polish in weeks.

Months."

Finn stiffened. "No, this is insane. Alternate realities? Other versions of ourselves? That's a sci-fi movie, Ro, not reality." He got up and knelt by the laundry basket to sift through the dirty clothes. "I'll show you the shirt and you'll see that I changed." He tossed clothes aside as he spoke. "I'm me. You're you. Everything is—where is that damn shirt?" He got up and crossed to the closet. "I threw it in here after I changed. It's got to—" Finn stood with his hands on his hips. "Maybe the bathroom."

"We checked. It's not there," I said quietly.

"Well, it has to be somewhere," he said, an edge of panic to his voice as he got down to look under the bed, then ripped the sheets and comforter off the top. I just sat and watched as he searched through the dresser drawers and the closet hangers. "I don't understand." He looked to me, lost and confused.

Then my phone rang.

I pulled it from my pocket, my breath catching when I saw who was calling.

"Who is it?" Finn asked.

I just held his gaze as I answered the call. "Hello?"

"Hi, I finally caught you." The connection was stronger than last time - still not crystal clear, but I could definitely recognize his voice.

Finn. *My* Finn.

"I'm, uh, going to put you on speaker. One sec." I switched on the speaker phone and set it on the bed between us as Finn sat down.

"Can you hear me okay?" I asked.

"Yeah. Everything all right?" I glanced at Finn, and he shook his head slightly. Like Lindsay, he couldn't hear the phone call either. He opened his mouth to speak, but I held a finger to my lips and nodded. He still looked wary, confused, but he kept silent and held my hand.

"Yeah, I'm fine," I said into the phone. "How's it going there?"

Finn sighed. "I miss you," he said, his voice weary. "Ro, I think I made a mistake."

Unscheduled Departure

"What do you mean?"

To say it was strange talking to Finn on the phone while he sat holding my hand would have been an understatement. Part of me felt like it was a betrayal, but I couldn't let go of him. In all of the bizarreness, he was somehow keeping me grounded.

"I spent the whole morning talking business and I hated every minute of it. I mean, I *hated* it," the Finn on the phone— my Finn— said. "I don't think I can do this, Ro."

I cleared my throat. "What are you going to do?"

"I don't know." He sighed again. "I'm going to talk to my mom about it. I think I'm going to tell her I changed my mind. She'll be pissed."

"You have to do what's right for you," I said quietly.

"Yeah. I just hate to disappoint her, you know?"

"I know." At my sad tone, Finn squeezed my hand.

"Well, I just wanted to hear your voice," my Finn said. "I'm going in to meet with her in a few minutes. I'll let you know how it goes."

When I realized he was going to hang up, I panicked. "Finn?"

"Yeah?"

"You'll call me back?"

He laughed. "Yeah, of course."

"Sorry." I tried to calm down. "It's just— there's something wrong with my phone and I can't call out right now."

"Oh, okay, yeah. I'll call you later."

"One more thing?"

"Yeah?" Finn's voice was quiet and fond. I felt a rush of emotion. God, I missed him.

"I know this sounds weird, but . . . " I chewed on my lip, my eyes on the phone. "Can you tell me something you've never told me before about yourself? Something only you would know?"

"What? Why?"

"Please?" How could I explain such a strange request? "Just anything. Please, Finn?"

It took a moment, but he finally answered my question,

told me he loved me, and promised he'd call again. I hung up and the room fell silent.

I took a deep breath. "When you were five years old you took your father's watch out of his dresser drawer," I said, my eyes focused on Finn's hand gripping mine. "You dropped it in the heater vent and couldn't figure out how to get it out. Your dad was so angry because he thought you'd been robbed, and you were too scared to tell him the truth. So you never did."

Slowly, ever so slowly, I lifted my eyes to Finn's face. He was pale, eyes wide with shock and disbelief, and he squeezed his eyes shut as he nodded once.

"Okay," he said once he'd regained his voice. "So how do we get him back?"

I scooted closer to him, unsure if the gesture would be welcome, but he reached out and pulled me close. I slipped my arms around his waist and rested my head against his chest.

"I don't know," I whispered. "But we'll have to figure out a way."

3:08 PM

As it turned out, the campus library had a pretty extensive section devoted to theories about alternate universes and multiple dimensions. Unfortunately, I found it difficult to make heads or tails of most of it. Lindsay joined us for the research session, relieved that Finn seemed to be on board, at least on some level. He was still quiet, though, stealing glances at me when he thought I wasn't looking. I assumed he was doing the same thing I had been— searching for more evidence, differences that separated me from the Rowan he knew.

The three of us sat at a table surrounded by books. Lindsay had her laptop open and was focused intently on a webpage, the tap of her fingernail on the mouse and the shuffle of turning pages the only sounds on the nearly-empty third floor.

"Listen to this," Finn said, running a finger along the

page in front of him. "*The Copenhangen interpretation holds to the premise that every event exists as a wave function, which contains every possible outcome of that event. The wave collapses once it is observed, in essence, creating reality. In other words, the observation of the event dictates the actual outcome, and all other realities are then eliminated.*"

"Of course," I muttered. "I say that all the time."

Finn shot me a mild glare, but kept reading. "*However, the Everett interpretation, also known as the Many Worlds Interpretation, holds that the wave function never collapses at all. Instead, it splits into a new world, and as a result there is a large - potentially infinite - number of universes, where every possible outcome of every situation has created a new reality.*"

"Whoa," Lindsay murmured. "So, there are who knows how many realities out there right now, where we're having this same conversation."

"Well, not the same one - it would have to be slightly different to create a new reality," Finn replied.

"So there's a Lindsay out there who decided to have tea instead of coffee this morning," she mused.

"Or to wear a blue shirt instead of a purple one," Finn said.

"Which is all very fascinating," I interjected, trying to keep the frustration out of my voice, but pretty much failing. "But none of this tells us how to get the Finn from this world back where he belongs." I glanced at Finn. "No offense."

"None taken."

"I think I might have something to help with that," Lindsay said, scooting closer and turning her laptop so we could see the screen.

I laughed. "Seriously, Linds? What the heck is quantum jumping?"

"Don't mock," she replied, sniffing indignantly. "Some of this stuff might seem a little out there, but it's the only thing I've found that even gives us a clue how to deal with this situation."

"Well, 'out there' kind of fits in this case," Finn added.

"Okay, okay fine." I held up my hands in surrender. "What does this Quantum Jumper have to say, whoever he is?"

"It's not a person, it's a theory," Lindsay said. "Basically, it builds on what Finn just read about multiple realities. Quantum jumping is traveling between those realities using various techniques like meditation and visualization."

"So, you're saying Finn just has to visualize the reality he wants to go to?"

Lindsay nodded. "Basically. I think it'll help to have them both revisit the place where they crossed over to begin with. And they'll both have to do the visualization."

Finn sat back in his chair. "Well, that might be easier said than done."

"I'm pretty sure the switch happened in the airport," I said. "And now the other Finn's all the way across the country." I couldn't imagine how we'd get them in the same place, let alone convince the other Finn— my Finn— to take part in what was quickly becoming a pretty insane-sounding plan.

"We could do the same thing," Finn suggested. "I could tell you another deep, dark secret to convince him."

"You know him better than me," I replied. "Would that work?"

He shrugged, "Couldn't hurt. I—"

My phone vibrated and bounced across the table, *Private Number* lighting up the screen. I scrambled to answer.

"Finn?"

"Hey." He sounded tired.

"How'd it go?" I could feel Finn and Lindsay watching me, the weight of their expectation and uncertainty heavy on my shoulders.

He gave a short laugh. "Well, I have good news and I have bad news."

"You know me. Bad news first, Finneapolis." I heard Other Finn's sharp intake of breath and glanced at him, feeling almost guilty.

"Not my name," my Finn said. "But the bad news is, my mother probably won't be inviting us for Christmas."

Unscheduled Departure

My heart started to pound in my chest. "And the good news?"

"I'm coming home."

I'm coming home.

Home.

"Home?" I whispered. "Like, here home? You're coming back?"

"I'm coming back." I could hear the excitement in his voice. "I never should have left."

I looked over at Finn, who was tapping a finger on the table, his knee bouncing beneath it. His grey eyes were dark, focused on me as he listened to my half of the conversation. I wondered if he knew what the other Finn was thinking— if he could imagine the road he took to get to this decision.

I had a feeling he could, since he'd arrived at the same place, although a little quicker.

"When?" I asked.

"I'll be on the last flight out tonight."

"Tonight?" My mind was whirling. Finn was coming back. He'd be at the airport.

"My flight gets in at 12:30 in the morning, your time."

I looked at the clock. Nine hours. He'd be at the airport in nine short hours. Which meant . . .

"Finn, there's something I need to tell you."

"What?" he replied, just as the other Finn leaned forward and hissed, "Wait."

"Um, hang on a sec," I told Finn-on-the-phone. "What is it?" I whispered.

"You don't need to tell him," Finn replied. "I have another idea."

I hesitated, glancing from him to the phone. "Are you sure?"

"You said it yourself, I know him best," he said. "And you don't have time to try and convince him of all of this if he's going to get on that plane." He reached out and grabbed my hand, squeezing it as he looked into my eyes. "Trust me."

I nodded slowly and pressed the phone back to my ear. "Finn?"

"Yeah, I'm here. What did you want to tell me?"

I ignored the worried pounding of my heart. "It's nothing. We can talk when you get here," I said.

I hoped.

"Tell him to call you as soon as he lands," Finn whispered.

I didn't ask why, but did as he said.

"Okay, babe," Finn-on-the-phone replied, and I could hear a happiness in his voice that had been missing for quite a while. "Can you pick me up?"

"Sure, yeah. No problem. I'll be there."

"Can't wait to see you. I love you, Ro."

"Me too," I whispered, turning away from the other Finn. "I'll see you soon."

"Bye."

I hung up and took a deep breath before turning back around. "Okay, so this better be some great idea," I said.

"Well, I don't know how great it is," Finn replied, "but I think it's the only shot we've got."

12:38 AM
Thursday

There was no way around it. We'd bought the cheapest tickets we could find—the red eye to Vegas—just to get around security. Still, I felt guilty...nervous...as we made our way through the scanners. Like we were getting away with something.

Which we were, but still.

Finn grabbed my hand as we quickened our pace... all but running as our steps echoed dully on the gleaming floor. An accident on the interstate delayed us almost an hour, and we got there just as Finn's plane touched down. As promised, he called me as soon as he landed, but it took some talking to get him to linger behind.

My text— the one that changed the other Finn's mind about leaving— had come through when he was standing on the jetway, waiting to board. We figured our best shot of switching them back was to get both Finns in the same spot —Lindsay said the veil must be thinner there. It was good

Unscheduled Departure

thing the incoming flight was landing at the same gate, or I didn't know what we would have done.

The airport was quiet at this time of night, and of those dazedly making their way around, nobody seemed to notice us. No one cared. We were just another couple of travelers rushing to get to the gate on time.

"Are you there?" My Finn's voice crackled out of the phone. "Ro, there aren't that many people left on the plane. I'm going to have to get off soon."

"I know," I replied through gasping breaths. I really needed to get in better shape. "I'm almost there."

"I don't understand—"

"I know you don't," I said, sliding around a corner. "Please, just trust me. In about two minutes, I need you to be in the same spot where you got my text."

He sighed. I knew he was tired.

"Finn?"

"Yeah, okay. I'll be there," he replied. "And you'll explain all of this when I see you, right?"

"I promise."

"Are you sure this is going to work?" Other Finn asked. I glanced at him.

Yes.

No.

"It'll work." We rounded a corner and I checked the time on my phone.

12:42. The screen wavered.

"Finn?" I clutched the phone to my ear desperately.

"I'm here. I'm waiting for you."

Waiting for me. Other Finn was watching me closely. I felt torn—guilty. I squeezed his hand and turned my attention to the gate signs overhead.

16...17...17a...18. Now for the fun part.

"How are you going to get past the desk?" Both Finns asked simultaneously. I fought an overwhelming urge to burst out in hysterical laughter.

"Good question." I all but slammed into the desk, startling the flight attendant focused on her computer. She pressed an open palm against her chest, fingernail clicking on her name tag. *Hi, I'm Rita. Come Fly with Me!* Rita opened her mouth to speak, but I beat her to it.

"I'm sorry," I said in a rush, willing my breathing to slow, my heart rate to calm, my smile to look a little more reassuring, a little less frenzied and maniacal.

The attendant's eyes widened and she took a nervous step backward.

Less maniacal.

"Rowan?" I wasn't sure which Finn spoke but I focused my attention on Rita..

"I'm so sorry," I said. "I think I dropped my bracelet when I got off the plane from . . ." I surreptitiously looked up at the arrivals board. ". . . Bismarck."

Rita's eyes narrowed with suspicion. "Lost and found is—"

"I checked already. No luck." I tried to look pathetic. I was pretty sure it wasn't a long trip. "Please, I just need to get on the jetway and look for it. I'll be quick, I promise," I said, not giving her a chance to interrupt me. "It was my grandmother's and it really means so much to me."

The woman still didn't look convinced, but she grabbed a pad of paper and a pen. "Perhaps you can describe the bracelet and I'll ch—"

"No!"

Rita jumped, her jaw twitching. I really needed to calm down.

The line of passengers emerging from the jetway doors slowed to a trickle. There wasn't much time left.

"I need to look," I said, forcing another pleading smile. "It's so small . . . delicate. You have to know what you're looking for."

"I'm sor—"

"Please. It'll only take a minute!"

Rita hesitated, almost like she was considering my request, then an older couple approached the desk, tickets in hand, and her face hardened.

"I'm sorry, but I can't allow unticketed passengers past the gate." She dismissed me by turning to the couple. "May I help you?"

Unscheduled Departure

I shoved my way in front of them, muttering apologies. "Please," I said, not averse to begging, "I need to get on that jetway."

"Miss, if you don't step back, I'm going to have to call Security," Rita replied. Another flight attendant, male and about six feet tall, took that moment to appear and glower at me over her shoulder.

I glanced through the open doors at the last few passengers disembarking from the plane.

"Rowan?"

I turned to walk away, Finn at my heels as I whispered into the phone. "They won't let me past the gate."

"What are we going to do? The flight attendants are headed this way. I can only pretend to fight with my carry-on for so long."

I scanned the area, desperate, panic trickling its way up my spine. I had to do something.

"Maybe we should just buy a ticket for the next flight," Other Finn suggested.

"There's no time," I murmured, a plan already forming as I watched Rita announce the boarding call for the adjoining gate, and passengers started to line up, dragging their carry-ons and crying children behind them.

"Get close to the door," I told Finn.

"What are you going to do?"

"Create a distraction."

"Ro—"

"Go!" I snapped. "We're almost out of time."

Finn chewed on his lip for a second, then nodded abruptly. I watched as he walked toward the windows and edged his way closer to the open doors leading to the jetway.

"Ro?"

"It's under control," I said quietly into the phone. "Be ready. He'll be there."

"Who?"

"One sec."

I took a deep breath to center myself, then strode up to a man in a black suit, grabbed his rolling carry-on, and turned to walk away.

"Hey!" he shouted.

I kept walking.

"Miss! Stop!"

I quickened my steps, looking over my shoulder only long enough to see Finn slip behind the barricade and through the doors.

"Go now!" I shouted into the phone. "Get to that spot, Finn— and think about how much you want to be home. How much you want to be with me."

"What?"

"Please, just do it," I said, dodging a stack of suitcases, then dropping the carry-on as I broke out into a run. "Think about me, Finn. Don't stop, okay?"

"Okay, I'm here. I'm at the spot," he said.

"Keep thinking of me," I replied, as two huge men in a golf cart with flashing lights sped toward me. "Don't stop, not matter what. I love you!" I hung up and hoped for the best.

I had to say one thing about security at Sea-Tac airport: They were fast. Efficient.

And strong as hell.

1:14 AM

I was a criminal.

I'd been detained and questioned, and had to explain that I had thought the man in the black suit had grabbed my luggage by mistake. It was so late and I was exhausted, and I was really sorry and I promised not to do it again if they'd just cut me a little slack this one time.

In the end, they released me, returned my bag and my phone, and escorted me to the doors with a repeated warning not to return to the airport anytime soon.

Oh yeah, and I was on the No-Fly List.

Perfect.

"Ro, are you okay?" Finn pushed off the wall and approached us, hesitating when the two officers holding my arms glared at him. "What are you doing with her?"

"Finn, it's okay," I said, searching his features as they dragged me along. I wanted to know if it worked— if he was my Finn, but I could hardly bring it up as I was being forcibly removed from the premises.

"Is this really necessary?" Finn asked, walking quickly alongside us.

Another glare, and Finn shrugged at me, cramming his hands in his pockets as we made our way to the parking garage. They let me go, watching with arms crossed and intimidation at an all-time high as we got into my car and drove slowly out of the garage. Once we hit open air, I checked my rear-view mirror and pulled over, turning to Finn.

I hesitated, unsure of how to proceed. If he was my Finn, he'd expect me to welcome him home. But if he was the other Finn . . .

He sighed. "It didn't work."

My heart sank.

"I made it onto the jetway," he said, "found the exact spot and visualized my ass off." He smiled when I snorted. "But nothing happened."

I slumped back into my seat, then stiffened. "Crap," I muttered, fumbling in my bag for my phone. The police had taken it and turned it off, and when I turned it back on, I winced when I saw four voicemails waiting for me. One was from Lindsay, wondering how things had gone. The other three, as expected, were from Finn, wondering where I was, and sounding progressively more irritated. He finally said he'd take a cab home and call me later.

I closed my eyes against frustrated and exhausted tears.

"You okay?" Finn asked gently.

"Not really."

It was quiet for a long moment, then I felt him take my hand. I looked over at him, blinking away the wetness in my eyes. "What are we going to do?" I asked.

He took a deep breath. "Get some sleep," he said. "And tomorrow, we'll figure it out."

It was several minutes before I nodded and pulled away from the curb.

1:57 AM

I drove in silence, both of us exhausted and frustrated as I navigated the all-but-abandoned freeway and took the exit to the U-District. I could feel Finn looking over at me now and then, but I didn't know what to say to him.

I pulled up to his apartment building and he cleared his throat.

"It's late," he said. He sounded nervous, unsure. It filled me with sadness. "You want to just stay here tonight?"

I nodded and turned off the car, unable to even summon the energy to form words. I followed him into the building, my feet dragging, scuffing along the sidewalk and kicking up rocks. We trudged up the stairs, ignoring the out-of-order elevator, and I felt the weight of every step, the urge to just lie down on the landing and go to sleep.

Finn took my hand without a word, and unexpected tears sprung up in my eyes.

What were we going to do? I didn't say it out loud, but it echoed in my head, over and over again. A question that had no answer. Or at least not an answer that I could face.

Finn was trapped in that other reality, and I was left with someone else. Someone so much like the man I fell in love with, but not him. Could I face a future with him? Or give him up for a relationship with a man I could only communicate with over an outdated cell phone?

Then there was the other me— another Rowan who, as far as I knew, had no idea that the Finn in her world wasn't really hers. I knew he would find her at some point, and couldn't keep down a hot rush of jealousy at the thought.

My head swam, tears trickling down my face as I bowed my head so Finn wouldn't see.

"Ro?" His voice was gentle. "It'll be okay."

I choked on a laugh. "How?"

He didn't answer, but unlocked the door and pulled me inside as my phone rang.

I jumped, scrambling for it in my bag, and let out a heavy breath when I saw it was Lindsay.

"Hello?" I collapsed onto Finn's couch.

Unscheduled Departure

"Hello? That's all you have to say is, 'Hello?'" Lindsay snapped. "I've been waiting here out of my mind. I knew I should have come with you."

"Yeah, then you could have been put on the No-Fly List too," I muttered.

"What? You're kidding!"

"I wish I was." I smiled in gratitude when Finn handed me a bottle of water. "But, long story short, no. It didn't work."

"Crap."

"Yeah."

"So . . . what now?"

I leaned back and closed my eyes, rubbing at my forehead. "I have no idea." I jolted and sat up. "Oh no, what's the date?"

"Umm . . . the thirteenth. Why?"

"Ugh." I collapsed onto my side and curled up in a ball. "I forgot to call my mom. Today— well, yesterday— was the anniversary of my dad's death. It's always tough on her."

I heard a gasp, but I wasn't sure if it was Lindsay or Finn, who was watching me from his own seat on the recliner.

"Linds?"

"You . . . " She took a shaky breath. "Did you say you're supposed to call your mom?"

"Well, yeah." I sat up, uneasiness trickling down my spine. "I thought I'd set a reminder on my phone, but with all the craziness I must ha—"

"Ro?" Lindsay was quiet. Finn stared at me, his mouth half-open, face pale.

"What is it?" I asked, not sure who I was talking to.

Lindsay replied, "Ro, you told me your mom died in a car accident when you were thirteen."

"What?"

"You don't like to talk about it much, but you said—"

"What are you talking about?" I shot to my feet, frantically searching the room for . . . . something. I didn't know what. "My mom lives in Salinas. She moved there after dad died to be closer to her sisters."

"Ro—" I hung up on Lindsay, not wanting to hear

anything more.

"Something's wrong," I muttered, scrolling through my contacts with shaking hands.

"What is it?" Finn asked.

"I think Lindsay's switched too," I said, cursing when I dropped the phone on the couch. I snatched it up and searched my contacts for my mother's number. "Where is it?"

"What are you looking for, Ro?" Finn's voice was quiet, tentative.

"My mom's number!" I all but shrieked, desperation racing through my veins, pounding and harsh. "Someone deleted her number."

"Ro—"

"No!" I shouted as the phone tumbled from my fingers, bouncing on the couch before it hit the floor. "Don't say it."

"Ro, she's gone. She died when you—"

"No," I screamed. "No, that's not right. No." Finn got up and took a step toward me and I held up my hands. "No!" I backed away . . . around the couch, down the hall. "No!" Into his bedroom and back, back, into the closet. They were wrong. They had to be wrong. How many of them were switched? More than Finn and Lindsay? What about the rest of my family? My other friends? What if nobody was who I thought they were?

I dropped to the floor and pulled in my knees, curled up on my side in the closet amidst Finn's— the *wrong* Finn's— shoes and discarded clothes. My mom was fine. She was alive. She was waiting for me to call, and probably would give me hell when—"

"Ro?"

It was Finn. The wrong Finn. The false Finn. But I didn't have to listen to him. This was wrong. It was all wrong.

Tears streamed down my face, dampening the carpet under my cheek as I clenched my eyes shut against the world, against the wrongness of it all.

"Rowan, please!"

I opened my eyes, the world blurry until I blinked, and the edge of the closet door came into focus, the corner of the chest of drawers, its wooden legs pressed into the carpet, and

Unscheduled Departure

... something stuffed underneath.

Something fabric. Something ... white.

I crawled forward a bit and reached out for it, Finn's voice fading to the background as blood rushed in my ears. I pulled out the mass of fabric and stared at it, my mind racing to make sense of what I was seeing.

A shirt.

A *white* shirt.

With a coffee stain on the cuff.

Finn dropped to his knees before me, hands twitching on his thighs like he wanted to reach out and touch me, comfort me, but didn't know if he was allowed.

"You found it," he whispered.

I nodded jerkily.

"That means . . . " I could hear him swallow and looked up to meet his gaze, drawing a heavy breath as I brushed the tears from my eyes.

"It means it's not you who's in the wrong place," I said, words raspy, as if struggling to leave my throat. "It's not you, and it's not Lindsay."

"Ro." He reached out to take my hand and I held it tightly, needing the comfort.

"It's me," I said finally.

"Yeah."

He tugged on my hand and I fell into his embrace, shuddering when he stroked my hair, murmuring words of consolation.

"I want to go home," I mumbled against his chest, the stained shirt still clutched in my fingers.

"I know." He pulled back and grabbed my shoulders, looking into my eyes. "We'll figure this out."

"How?"

"Finn will call in the morning."

"Maybe," I muttered. "He's pretty angry at me for not meeting his flight."

"He's going to figure out something's wrong when he sees you— the other you," Finn clarified, shaking his head. "He'll track her down and when she has no idea what he's talking about, he'll figure it out. He'll figure it out and he'll call."

"Then what?"

He shrugged. "I think we had the right idea the first time— just the wrong people. We try it again, with you and the other Rowan. But to do that . . ." He winced when he met my gaze.

"Crap," I mumbled.

"Yeah," he said, sitting back on his heels. "We've got to go back to the airport."

12:21 PM

First, we had to wait for Finn to call. After another nearly-sleepless night, we sat on Finn's couch, pretending to watch daytime television between bouts staring at my cell phone. Lindsay showed up after her last class, bearing takeout and another pile of books on cross-dimensional travel, so I poked at my Thai noodles and half-heartedly flipped through pages of *Shifting Realities*.

It wasn't until early afternoon that it finally happened, and I grabbed the phone, filled with a mixture of relief and dread.

"Hello? Finn?"

"Ro, what the hell is happening?"

It was embarrassing that it had only taken Finn about ten minutes in the other Rowan's company before he realized something was terribly, terribly wrong. And it had been him, not me— the other me, God, this was confusing— who'd called Lindsay and come to the same conclusion that we had. Similar to my experience, no one else in his reality could hear me over the phone, and I couldn't hear them. There was just this weird connection between Finn and me, my last tether to my own world.

"So what do we do?" he asked.

"You need to get . . . Rowan— the name felt thick and strange on my tongue— to the airport," I said, a rush of images filling my mind: a support column, a black scuff mark on industrial tile . . . a text message wavering before my eyes.

A rush of dizziness that now meant so much more than I

could have imagined.

"Tell her she needs to go to the spot by the security line where she texted you when you left," I said.

Other Finn leaned in. "How are you going to—"

I held up a hand. "It's going to be tricky on my end," I told my Finn. "We're going to have to time this perfectly. It's almost 12:30, so, let's say two o'clock on the dot. She has to be there at two. And she has to be focused on getting home— getting home to *her* Finn. *Her* world. *Her* friends." But not her family. She had no family. "Call me when you're in place," I told Finn before hanging up.

Guilt twisted in my stomach. "Should I have told Finn to tell her? That my mom is alive?"

Lindsay shook her head sadly. "You can't, Ro. It would only make it more difficult for her."

"But she could have seen her one last time. Said goodbye, maybe?"

"It would only have made it harder for her to leave," Finn said.

Lindsay nodded, reaching out to take my hand. "It's not just that," she said. "Everything I've read says we're on borrowed time, here. There's no telling how long the passage you used will even be there— if it still is."

I knew as she said it, that Lindsay was right. Still.

"I just feel so badly for her," I said. "It must have been horrible."

Lindsay sighed. "It was. But Ro, she dealt with it a long time ago. She's okay, now. Don't make it worse for her out of your own guilt."

I took a deep breath and stood up, letting Lindsay go. "Okay, then. We need to get to the airport, and I need to hang out by the security line without drawing attention to myself, or getting flagged as a potential terrorist." I looked at both of them expectantly. "Suggestions?"

1:50 PM

"We're in position," Finn said, his voice clearer than ever over the phone. I hoped that was a good sign. "Security's side-eying us a little, but no problems so far."

I nodded at Lindsay in the rearview mirror as she circled the airport dropoff again. We figured it was safer than trying the parking garage. I adjusted my sunglasses and blonde wig, hoping the disguise would be enough.

"We're on our way," I said, checking out the security guards posted at the entrances. "There, Linds." I pointed over her shoulder at an empty spot at the curb.

She pulled over and grabbed my wrist before I could leave. "Good luck," she said.

I nodded and hugged her over the seat. "See you soon. Thank you," I whispered.

We got out of the car and Finn grabbed the empty suitcase we'd brought along to try and fit in. I held his hand firmly as we walked across the sidewalk and through the sliding glass doors. We both tensed as we stepped off the escalator and the ticket counters came into view. Finn squeezed my hand and we forced ourselves to smile at each other and make small talk as we passed the security guards manning the luggage checking station.

They didn't spare us a second glance.

So far, so good.

1:58 PM

"Well?" Finn glanced over his shoulder nervously. "Where is it?"

"I . . . I don't know," I replied, circling back to the edge of the security line, then pacing back to the wall. "There was a black scuff, but they must have waxed the floors or something."

I looked up at the support posts and lifted the phone to my ear. "Is she sure she's in the right spot?" I asked.

I heard a rustle on the phone, Finn talking to the other me, then he said, "Yeah. She says there's a scuff on the floor."

"Well, it's gone here." I looked up at the posts again. "I think it's this one," I murmured.

"Trust your instincts," Finn said, touching my shoulder.

I swallowed down a rush of nerves and leaned against the

Unscheduled Departure

post as I had when I'd sent the text. A movement at the corner of my eye caught my attention, and I spotted a security officer looking my direction and speaking into his radio.

I looked down quickly and cursed under my breath.

"What is it?" Finn asked. Both Finns asked.

"I think I've been spotted," I said quietly. "We've got to do this now."

There were two officers watching now— no, three— and not only watching, but approaching in a wide circle. I closed my eyes and tried to focus, to think of home . . . Finn . . . my mother.

Finn mumbled something under his breath and my eyes flew open. He leaned in and kissed me. "Good luck," he whispered, and he whirled around and took off at a run, slamming into one of the officers and knocking him to the floor. The others took off in pursuit.

"Finn!" I shouted.

"Go!" he shouted back, and I closed my eyes and tried to do just that. Tried not to worry about what would happen when the other Rowan emerged, her boyfriend now joining her on the No-Fly list.

I owed her an apology.

"Tell Rowan I'm sorry," I murmured over the phone.

"For what?" Finn replied.

"She'll see." I closed my eyes. "I don't know if this is going to work, Finnefred."

"Lame," he said, laughter in his voice. "You can do better."

I smiled, focusing on his voice. "Car-Finn Miranda?"

He snorted. "Try again."

I thought of Finn— of the first time I met him, in line at the dining hall. Of our first date at a horrible Greek restaurant that he'd picked, trying to impress me. Of our first kiss after he'd bought me the most amazing ice cream cone to make up for it.

"Finnick Odair?"

"You've used that one before."

A swirl of images flooded my mind, one after the other in rapid succession: Finn's smile, his touch, the sound of his laughter . . . the taste of his kiss. I leaned into the post, a rush of dizziness hitting me suddenly.

"Finn?"

"I'm here. Try again."

I thought of that little scar on the corner of Finn's mouth, the way he slowed his steps so I could always keep up.

The first time he told me he loved me, and he picked up my hand, pressing his lips to the tip of my finger, saying he always wanted it to point toward home.

Toward him.

"Finn-tendo sixty-four?"

Finn laughed, louder than expected. "Now you're talking," he said.

And I realized I hadn't heard it through the phone. In fact, I wasn't even holding my phone anymore.

I opened my eyes to see Finn leaning against the same post, right in front of me. He looked at his phone and shrugged, stuffing it into his pocket.

"Guess we got disconnected," he said, laughter in his eyes.

I threw myself at him, wrapping my arms around his neck as I inhaled his scent and he held me tight.

"Welcome home," he said.

1:06 PM
Friday

I walked out of the building after my World Religions midterm and blinked at the bright sunshine as I headed toward the coffee shop to meet Finn for lunch. I studied the faces of the people I passed, more than I ever had before, and I wondered how many of them were where they belonged.

I'd thought about it a lot since everything happened. It was hard to think of anything else, really. What led to me crossing over into that other world? Was it something I did? Or did my indecision about whether or not to beg Finn to stay create a middle-ground somehow, a way for me to live in both worlds for a moment, until I finally dropped into the other one?

Unscheduled Departure

I supposed I'd never know.

And I tried not to think about the other possibility: that we all, every one of us, were just floating along, sliding from reality to reality, with no idea at all that it was happening. That every time our hair stood on end, telling us something was wrong— or we were struck with a sense of déjà vu or an inexplicable hunch— it was really a sign of us shifting between worlds.

Or the world shifting between each of us.

I walked into the diner and saw Finn sitting at a table in the back, his face lighting up when he spotted me, and I couldn't help it— I checked the length of his hair, the curve of the scar on the corner of his mouth, counted the crinkles at the corners of his eyes as he smiled.

I doubted I could ever look at him again and not feel compelled to check and make sure he was my Finn. But how could I know for sure? And in the end, what did it really matter? If our choices create our world, then wouldn't any Finn be my Finn?

"Ro? You okay?" his voice jolted me out of my circular thoughts and I leaned down to kiss him, just to make sure.

Nope. Not weird at all.

"Yeah, I'm fine," I said with a smile. "Everything's good."

My phone rang and I pulled it from my bag as I slipped into the seat across from him. The smile froze on my face at the sight of the words flashing on the screen.

Private Number.

No.

"What's wrong?" Finn asked, tilting his head to try and see my phone. "Who is it?"

My thumb hovered over the accept button for a moment, then I glanced up at Finn and set the phone on the table, turning it so he could read it. His eyebrows shot up and he looked at me expectantly. Waiting.

"Probably a telemarketer," he said.

"Yeah."

"Or a wrong number."

"Could be."

The ringing continued, the electronic melody combining with a vibration that bounced my phone a little across the tabletop.

"So, what are you going to do?" he asked, reaching for my hand.

I held on tight, took a deep breath, and answered the call.

If you enjoyed *Unscheduled Departure*, check out the **MORE Trilogy** by T.M. Franklin!

They're gifted. They're powerful. And they're after her.

Ava Michaels isn't sure what's real anymore. She's haunted by terrifying nightmares of a huge, hulking man with mismatched eyes. But then that same man shows up on her doorstep and tries to abduct her – and her mild-mannered physics tutor, Caleb Foster, appears out of nowhere to come to her defense.

And she has no idea why.

On the run for her life, Ava discovers a secret, ancient race with amazing gifts and abilities. But they see her as a threat, and now her life is on the line. She can't hide forever, and must find a way to survive – with or without Caleb's help.

Along the way, Ava learns she's not really normal. In fact, she's not simply human.

She's a little bit MORE.

MORE is the first book in a complete, action-packed trilogy. If you like heart-stopping adventure, awesome supernatural abilities, kick-butt heroines, and a touch of romance, then you'll stay up all night flipping the pages of T.M. Franklin's MORE Trilogy.

And don't miss **The New Super Humans!**

A supernatural house. A terrifying vision. The Order must embrace frightening powers to take down an unspeakable evil.

Chloe Blake's campus rental has it all: a retro Victorian vibe, a beautiful picture window, and a perfect view of her cute fratboy crush. But when she sees disturbing visions of death slide across the panes, she's convinced she's glimpsed into her crush's future. She'll stop at nothing to change fate and save him… even if it means the whole campus will think she's crazy.

Wren Galloway has lost track of all the crummy cities she's lived in. Plagued by night terrors, Wren wakes in a cold sweat with the vision of a nearby Victorian house still in her mind… and a strong urge to seek out the powerful talisman calling out to her from its attic.

Drawn together by an ancient force, Chloe and Wren must work together to discover the house's secrets and unlock their hidden powers to take down the shadowy specter that haunts their premonitions and leaves death in its wake.

Super Humans is the first book in **The New Super Humans**, an edge-of-your-seat contemporary fantasy series. If you like original magic systems, startling suspense, and fast-paced action, then you'll love TM Franklin's riveting thrill ride.

Get more information at TMFranklin.com
Or join T.M. Franklin's mailing list for the latest on new releases, sales, and giveways at
Bit.ly/TMFranklinSubscribe

Made in the USA
Lexington, KY
28 May 2018